IN THE
MOONLIGHT

R.L. NELSON

Randee Nelson

Contents

For my Aunt Noreen and Uncle Dave,
If it weren't for you, I never would have
known the joy of story-telling.
Thank you.

IN THE MOONLIGHT

I

The Edge of Midnight

It's midnight, it's freezing, and I'm covered in blood.

I inch closer to the fire next to me, attempting to warm myself, but as I do so I feel another splatter of blood hit my back. The cold liquid slides down my neck and spine, causing my whole body to shiver. I am covered in it, this concoction of corn syrup and red food dye. My white shirt is now red, and my denim jacket and jeans are splattered; but I'm mostly regretting wearing my favorite pair of white vans, they are beyond salvageable.

Blood-Fest was the last place I ever wanted to be. A desert rave, an hour away from all civilization on Halloween weekend sounded like the perfect setup to a horror movie, but I was outvoted three to one. I'm sitting at the bonfire by myself now, almost fifty feet away from the crowd of dancers gathered in front of the DJ booth. Across from me, on the other side of the fire are a group of friends laughing. A smiley boy talks to a blonde girl, while a girl with flowers in her hair kisses the cheek of a boy in a teal beanie. I become transfixed on them, lost in the moment, no one showing them a care in the world. Unapologetically themselves. I find myself wishing that could be me; *us*. With Gabby wrapped in Andrews arms, Jess and I making fun of them for how publicly they love each other, and Aph beaming because it's nearly impossible to find your soulmate and they found each other. But no. Andrew is gone, Gabby is depressed, and Jess and I only get along for Gabby's sake.

I can't look at them anymore.

I stand up and make my way to the dance floor, away from the fire and my wishes of a normal life. I make my way through the dense crowd of "blood" covered people, get shot by the water guns loaded with the fake blood a few more times and over to the side of the dance floor where only a small crowd of people are standing off to the side exchanging bracelets.

I find the girls easily, Gabby sees me and waves me over, I shake my head and she nods before grabbing Jess and Aphrodite by their wrists to drag them over to me. They too are covered in fake blood.

"I'm beat, you guys ready to go home?" Gabby winks at me, her pupils are huge, a smile spreading across her face.

"Yeah, I was over this hours ago" Jess rolls her eyes and crosses her arms, Aphrodite nods.

"Let's get outta here." I say and link arms with the girls.

We force our way out of the crowds of people and onto the dirt road that'll take us back to the car. There are still people showing up, girls in tutus with glow sticks around their arms and necks, boys in all kinds of costumes and shouting random things. Aph grips my hand tighter as we pass a larger group of boys who seem to be eyeing us. I steer us around them and we make our way to the car, an old red Ford Escape that Gabby inherited when she got her license. I quickly start the car and turn on the heater as the other girls file in. We sit and shiver in silence for a moment as the car heats up and more cars line up on the road. Aph sits in the passenger seat and Jess and Gabby cuddle up in the back for warmth.

"I brought a blanket, it's in the back." I tell Gabby and she reaches over the seat to pull it out before wrapping Jess and herself in it. I take a deep breath and put the car into drive, look both ways and pull out onto the dirt road that leads us out. The road was abandoned for a long time before we came out here, it has huge rocks and damage from the rains causing the car to bounce and squeak. Coins rattle in the cup holders, filling the car with noise. We make our way down the road for miles, I do my best to follow the traffic cones that mark the way out to the main highway.

As soon as the tires hit the smooth asphalt of the main road, the world around us gets quiet. Any noise coming from the car is now muted and I'm left to my own thoughts as we begin the hour and a half drive home to Paradise. The rave was barely a distraction from myself, I still couldn't get Andrew out of my head. I've been having nightmares about him for the last three months, of course it wouldn't have been that easy, but images of him being torn apart by monsters repeatedly haunt me. I left him behind in the underworld six months ago, attended his fake funeral five months ago, and became friends with his soul-mate four months ago. I tried to do what everyone told me, just focus on the real world, got my driver's license, went to summer school to fix my grades, helped Nix acclimate to life in Paradise. But none of it really helped, it just made me feel guilty. Guilty for being here, for living, for trying to have a real life, guilty for leaving my best friend in hell.

I watched Gabby go through the same feelings as I did, but she didn't know the truth and that killed me. I couldn't tell her that he was still alive, trapped in the Underworld with the Greek God of death, couldn't tell her that it was my fault he was there in the first place, so I stayed by her side through all of it. All the tears and the screaming. At first it shocked me that she felt so hurt, I didn't know that they'd been as close as they were. But they were soulmates after all, and that counted for a lot. One day we became inseparable, all the crying was done, and we came out stronger because of it. Of course, Jessica was still there, we got along for the sake of Gabby, although it wasn't as hard as I thought it would be. Jessica and I were friends before I lost my memory, she had just been hurt that I couldn't remember her and that hurt turned to hate turned to mutual friendship.

Aphrodite wormed her way into our lives about three and a half months ago. Ares had dumped her, and she wanted to know what it felt like to be human. Dad assumed that accepting a God into our home was fitting, given that it was the reason we were wolves in the first place. He turned the basement into an apartment, and she's been living with us ever since. Of course, she couldn't just go by her real identity, so she came up with a new one: Daphne Onassis, our seventeen-year-old cousin from

California. Instead of looking like a twenty-five-year-old bomb-shell, she changed her outwards appearance to reflect her new identity too, although she still relatively looks the same to me. Because of that, I've almost called her Aphrodite too many times in front of Gabby and Jess, so I've taken to calling her Aph for short.

"Did you love him?" Gabby asks quietly, snapping me out of my thoughts. We've been driving for almost a half an hour at this point, I'd assumed I was the only one still awake. I look at her in the rear-view mirror and find that she is staring at me. Her once long blonde hair is now jet black and cut short, making her bright green eyes look all the brighter in the city lights. Her hair was one of the many changes that came from the "death" of Andrew.

"Who?" I ask her.

"Areon." She states, she hasn't stopped staring and I can feel the blush on my cheeks as she says his name. That is the one thing we never talk about, or rather, the one person we didn't talk about. She doesn't know that he's a God, doesn't know that he manipulated her memories about him. All she knows is that Areon moved far away from here. If only she knew how far.

It's not that I didn't want to talk about him, I do, but I couldn't talk about him with Gabby and I sure as hell didn't want to talk about him with Aph or Jessica. But did I love him? Do I love him? I'm not sure. Do I miss him? All the time. It wasn't love, but it wasn't nothing either. Part of my new-found insomnia is due to the amount of time I spent wondering if he was thinking of me. Wondering if he misses me like I miss him.

I've spent hours going over every interaction I'd ever had with him. The hand holding, the kisses, the times he cradled me in his arms when I was hurt. But if this is love, then I don't want it. I don't want to give him the power to destroy me more than he already has.

"No." I tell her flatly. Aphrodite shifts in her seat, obviously not asleep. I fight the urge to glare at her.

"You're lying." Gabby states without hesitation, my face flushes.

"How do you know?"

"I saw the way you looked at him. It was the same way I looked at Andrew." His name hangs in the air, and I once again find myself wanting to tell her the truth. To tell her that Andrew isn't dead, just living in the Underworld. But I can't do that without spilling Aph's and the other Gods secret, not without breaking the golden rule that humans can't know about the existence of the Gods or there will be war. Instead of saying anything I fill the car with as much sound as I can, flipping the heater on higher and blasting whatever radio station Gabby's mother has on the first preset. Gabby seems to get the message and turns back to the window.

By the time I pull into my driveway, the sun hasn't even risen. Aph and I split up, she takes the back entrance to the basement, and I take the front door.

I wish I would have gone with her.

"Do you even know what time it is?" Deme scowls at me in the doorway.

"Good morning." I say avoiding her question, it only makes her angry.

"Rose, I was worried." She looks at my blood-covered clothes, "Is that blood?"

"It's fake. Sorry, next time I guess I'll text." I brush past her and go for the stairs.

Home is the last place I want to be. Nothing has been the same since Phoenix and I returned from the Underworld. Phoenix slipped into his old life easily even though he was technically a second-year senior and I struggled. It wasn't his fault, he was popular, he has more friends than he had before he left and is the star of the football team. I am constantly tired, and only hang out with Gabby and Aph; Jessica barely hangs out with us anymore, tonight was the first time I'd seen her in weeks

"The curse. The moon. The blood will run." Deme whispers. I turn to question her, but she has already hit the floor. I rush back down the stairs to her side; Dad runs out of his room and meets me.

"What did she say?" He asks too calmly. Demes eyes have rolled to the back of her head, and she is shaking. "Rose, what did she say?" He asks again, more sternly. I can smell alcohol on his breath.

"She said 'The curse. The moon...'" I can't help but stare at Deme's writhing body on the floor. I feel my dad's hand on my shoulder and catch his glare. "The curse. The moon. The blood will run." I finally get out in a panic, "What does it even mean?"

"Nothing, go to your rooms. Both of you." He says and I notice Nix is now at the bottom of the stairs, "Don't answer the door either, no matter who you *think* it is."

"But—" I start but Dad shushes me and pulls Deme into his arms.

"I don't want to hear it, Rose. Go to bed." He sighs at me and disappears behind the living room door. I glance at Nix, but he only shrugs and goes to his room, locking the door behind him. I follow suit and lock my bedroom door behind me.

I wake up late in the afternoon. The sun tries to enter my room through a crack in my curtains and downstairs, my family doesn't even attempt to keep quiet. I can hear the news on in the living room and dishes clanking around in the kitchen. I roll over and look at my phone. Nothing. Not like I thought my phone would be blown up with notifications, I deleted most of my social media a couple of months ago. Somehow, seeing a bunch of kids pretend to know Andrew on the internet, turned me off the whole concept. I roll back over and stare at the ceiling while listening to the sounds of life beneath me.

I would've fallen asleep again if it weren't for my father's heavy footsteps on the stairs. Not even a moment later, he's banging at my door.

"Enough is enough, Rose, it's time to get up." He demands from the other side of the door. "We need to discuss something as a family." I roll my eyes as I listen to his footsteps retreat down the hall. Family discussions usually involve the rest of them brainstorming ideas to make me happy.

This should be no different.

Phoenix, Deme, and I are squished together on the couch in front of my fathers' chair. We've been sitting here for ten minutes waiting for dad to say something, but he only stares at the three of us.

"This has been fun and all, but—," I start getting up from the couch.

"Don't even think about getting up from that couch, Rose." Dad interrupts me. His voice is stern, so I sit back down.

"Sorry," I mutter.

"I'm sure you will be." If looks could kill, I'd be buried by now.

"Dad, why are we all here?" Phoenix asks.

"We need to discuss your sister," I roll my eyes, I knew it. "I know that the two of you witnessed what happened last night, and I believe it is time I tell you the truth." He considers his next words very carefully. "Phoenix, Rose, you both inherited the wolf gene. I told both of you that Deme was lucky and did not receive this trait. She did, however, receive a different trait." He says and I must look visibly confused. Wasn't this discussion supposed to be about my attitude or something?

"What are you saying?" I ask.

"Your mother was an oracle." Dad states. Phoenix looks just as confused as I feel.

"What does that even mean?" Phoenix asks.

"It means that your mother had visions of the future. Her family comes from a long line of Oracles. There are only seven Oracles in the world, your mother was one of them, but there can only ever be seven. When Deme was born, your mother had a vision that she would take her place as the seventh Oracle and as Deme's power grew stronger, your mother would grow weaker." The pain in his eyes is so unbearable that I can't look at him. "Your mother got sick because her power was being drawn from her. The same thing will happen to Deme, should she choose to have children of her own." Dad wipes his face with his hands, and I need to wipe the tears from my own eyes. I look at Deme, she is sobbing quietly in between Phoenix and me.

"Is there some way that she can give it up?" I ask desperately.

"If there were, your mother would still be here today." Dad says halfheartedly. I stare at him in disbelief.

I risked *everything* to keep her safe.

I lost Andrew, to keep her safe.

"What if she doesn't have kids?" Phoenix asks. His expression blank.

"She will live forever, slowly aging for eternity." Dad says. I can't hear anymore; an annoying ringing has taken up all the space in my ears. Before I even know what I'm doing, I stand up and head for the door. "Where are you going?" Dad asks.

"I don't know, Gabby needs her car back. I'll be home later." I tell him, slamming the door behind me. Within minutes I'm driving down the road.

This is all too much to handle.

Not only have I failed at saving my best friend, but I failed at saving my little sister too. I assumed that freeing the wolves would have ended any threats from Hades and she would remain safe. I assumed wrong; Hades wasn't even what I should have been worrying about.

I can't save her from this.

And what kind of way is that to live; knowing you'll die, your kids never getting to see you grow old or slowly age forever? What would I do? I haven't given it much thought considering its highly likely that I will be passing down my own messed up genetics if I decide to have kids, but to live forever watching everyone you love grow old and die. I would never want that fate. I'd surely end it all.

But Deme isn't me.

The roads blur together as I make my way to Gabby's house. I didn't even tell her I was on my way to return the car. But maybe that's a good thing. She'll be able to tell that something is bothering me, and I can't tell her about Deme without telling her every other secret that I've kept from her. With every passing day, it gets harder to keep things from her.

It would be so easy to tell Gabby everything. To spill every secret, tell her everything is a lie, but she would never forgive me. *I wouldn't forgive me.* I've gone over this situation in my head a million times, and every time the outcome is the same. I've lied to her for too long, kept Andrews fate a secret for too long, to remain friends with her. No. Not telling her is much easier than ruining her life.

Ares wouldn't be very forgiving either. If I told Gabby the truth, I'd be risking the life of every single God. Humans can't know of their existence, it's their second most important rule. The first being, that the Gods can't meddle in the affairs of humans either, although that circles back to the second rule. If they were to help the humans or interfere in our lives, it would be game over. Every single God would be killed until Ares was the only one left. I'm honestly not too sure why he hasn't just killed them anyway. The first time I'd met Ares, he didn't seem too keen on the other Gods. I mean he even broke up with

Aphrodite, why wouldn't he want to be the last God left in the world?

I leave Gabby's car in her driveway and place the keys in a flowerpot by her front door. I wait to text her until I reach the woods across from her house and hide behind a tree. I wait and watch as she opens the door. She looks excited to see me and then disappointed when she realizes that I didn't stick around to hang out. I watch as she picks the keys out of the flowerpot and smells one of the red flowers sitting in the planter. She looks around again, probably wondering how I left so quickly without her seeing, but she drops the thought and heads back inside, gently closing the door behind her.

Turning has become second nature to me now. I can transform into a wolf and back without even blinking and the pain is completely gone. Although, I haven't been transforming much lately due to the amount of time I have been spending with Gabby. I find myself running a familiar path, to a place that I haven't been to in a long time. The same familiar smells cloud my nose and I feel at home. I'm not sure why I've been holding back coming here for so long.

I turn the corner and come to a welcoming sight. The small building that was once my childhood fort still stands where it always has. The trees are now a beautiful shade of orange and red, leaving the old rotting building looking almost magical, like an old witch's cottage. I haven't been here in months, I almost brought Gabby out here a few times, but it felt wrong. It felt like I was betraying Andrew and Areon by coming out here with someone new. I needed to be here today though. I needed my old friends, even if they aren't actually here with me.

Now that I am alone, I want to scream. After all this time, I still can't save Andrew. I can't save my sister, and I couldn't save my mother. Is everyone in my life going to end up leaving me? Would it be easier if I left them first? My mind is racing with questions I'll never be able to answer. I think back to night we destroyed Andrew's truck. I was so mad at Areon for wanting to erase my memory, but would it have been so bad? To forget Andrew and everything that happened. Would it have been easier to cope with his disappearance if I hadn't known that I caused it? He tried to come see me again at Andrews funeral, and I only pushed him further away. I wouldn't even listen to anything he had to say. The heartbroken shock on his face is how I see him in my memories now. If only I listened to him, heard him out, maybe I wouldn't feel so alone now.

Rain begins to pour down from the skies like a thick black blanket of clouds is being placed over me. Small amounts of rainwater drip down through the ceiling and splash onto the old floorboards. The sounds calm me down a bit. There is nothing I can do right now, so why should I worry about it. Deme is only fifteen, she still has years before she has to start worrying about having kids with someone. Maybe by then I can find a cure for her. I take a deep breath. *Petrichor.* I can almost hear Andrew telling me this word, followed by the definition of it. The smell of rain after a long period of dry weather. No matter how many times I'd heard the word before, Andrew always told me what it meant. This alone has the power to make me tear up. I feel guilty.

Guilty that it's been too long since he left, guilty that he can't be here to smell it with me. The building suddenly feels cold and eerie, and I feel a little too lonely.

I make sure to get home before dinner, even though I would have much rather stayed at the fort all night. The overwhelming feeling of Deme's fate weighs heavily on my shoulders, and it's obvious that everyone else feels the same. I don't hear a single word from the kitchen as Deme and Dad cook around each other. I guess all the time that I was gone, this became normal for them. Making something new every night was a good way to keep our father from relapsing on alcohol. Although, He still sneaks a couple shots in when he thinks no one is watching him; I'll never tell him that I know.

As we dig into our home-made enchiladas, none of us say a word to each other. The scraping of our forks against the plates screams in my ears. The tension in here is so thick, a knife couldn't even cut through it.

"What did you do today, Rose?" Deme asks me, breaking the silence.

"I took Gabby's car back to her." I tell her.

"How did you get home?" She asks.

"I walked," I shrug.

"That's a far walk." She says.

"Not when you're a wolf." I laugh. No one laughs with me.

"How are we supposed to pretend that nothing happened this morning? Like you didn't just tell us our sisters jacked up fate." Phoenix spits.

"There is no need to pretend, Nix. If you'd like to talk about it, then all you needed to do was bring it up." Dad tells him.

"We need to decide this as a family," Nix says, "We need to figure out what Deme is going to do." I glance at her and she sinks into her chair before pushing her plate away.

"I believe she will have a family one day and pass on her gift, as your mother did." Dad tells us.

"No! She shouldn't pass this on, she will die!" Nix yells, "I won't let her kill herself."

"She's fifteen." I state.

"What?" Nix turns his anger on me.

"She's still only a kid. It doesn't matter what she does, she is my sister, and I will support her no matter the decision she makes." I tell him calmly.

"So, you'll just let her die?" He questions me.

"If that is what she decides, Nix. The choice is hers and hers alone. We can't decide for her." I answer, he glares at me, but I don't react.

"You're right, Rose." Dad speaks up. He changes the subject to something else, although I'm not paying much attention to what he's saying. I glance at Deme, she's not paying much attention to the conversation either, but she looks up and smiles at me quickly before she starts picking at her food again.

We sat at the dinner table for almost an hour before I head down to the basement to see Aph. We never used it much, but the basement was sort of like an extra living room for us, we spent most of our time down here playing video games on an old box tv. The tv is still down here, although it's covered in about three inches of dust now. We put a bed down here for Aph when she first moved down here, along with a mini-fridge and an old microwave. Although, I don't think she's touched either yet, the tables are littered with old take-out boxes. I'm not entirely certain why she lives with us, she must be rich enough to afford the best hotels and maybe even purchase a few mansions.

"I heard your sisters' powers are awakening." Aph says to me as I plop down into the couch. Her long blonde hair is up in a messy bun and she's wearing an oversized shirt. If she weren't so over-the-top beautiful, you'd never know she was a God.

"Yeah, it caused quite the family fight." I tell her.

"As it should, being an Oracle is no small feat." She says.

"I'd rather talk about anything else."

"Alright then, want to watch something?" She asks, turning on the small flatscreen in front of the couch.

"I don't care, you pick." I tell her. She flips the channel to the news and the screen fills with images of protesters. We watch together as the news anchor reports about the latest Black Lives Matter protests. As the scene changes to some footage of the protests, Aph gasps and pauses the screen.

"No way!" She exclaims.

"What? What is it?"

"That's Athena!" She tells me as she points to the screen. She points out a younger looking woman towards the front of the group. Her mouth is open from yelling, and I can't point out any particular features through the screen, but I'm sure she's just as beautiful in person as she is on the tv. She is tall and slim from what I can tell, she towers over most of the other people around her, and there is a golden band wrapped around her head creating a contrast between her dark hair and the band itself.

"I thought you guys couldn't meddle. What is Athena doing at a protest?" I ask.

"She's doing what she does best. Fighting for what she believes in. I'd hardly call it meddling. Since she isn't forcing people to do what she wants." Aphrodite explains, she hasn't taken her eyes off the screen though. I can't help but feel like she wants to be right there next to her.

"Do the other Gods feel the same way?" I ask her.

"Feel the same way about what?"

"The rule against meddling. Do they wish they could? Clearly Athena and you do, I would think Are—I mean Zagreus wishes you guys could too." I explain.

"That's a very complicated question with an equally complicated answer." She thinks for a moment, "There are just so many of us, and I can't speak for us all."

"I don't understand how Ares could have taken all of you down though. It just doesn't make sense to me, you're all immortal."

"There are ways to destroy a person without killing them." Aph looks off into the distance, "But Ares wasn't alone in his battle. He was angry, furious that Zeus looked at him as nothing but a weakling. Phobos, Deimos, Eris, and Enyo wreaked havoc on us. One by one we were defeated until Olympus fell. When Ares finally got to Zeus, they were at a stalemate. Zeus demanded peace, but Ares would only agree under one condition, No God shall interfere with the world from that point on, or all of us would be killed. You know which Zeus chose." She looks back at me, her eyes as hard as stone.

"Wait, Ares would have killed you? I thought you were together."

"We were. Back then, things were much more tense. It seemed like we were fighting battle after battle, war after war. The other Gods looked down on us for choosing to be together, I am a married woman after all." She rolls her eyes.

"You're married?!"

"Against my wishes, yes. I was given to Hephaestus by Zeus himself." She laughs, "Arranged marriages were a big thing back then."

"So, why not meddle now? It doesn't seem like you have much to lose." I ask.

"If I could meddle, I don't know if I would." Aphrodite tells me.

"What do you mean?"

"Everything is already so messed up, introducing the world to their soulmates might create more heartbreak. There are some people who are happy out there, with families and children. I'd be tearing families apart, destroying lives. The same could be said for the other Gods as well," She points at Athena on the screen again. "We help where we can, but the world is already so different that we wouldn't know if we were doing the right thing or not anymore."

"I guess that makes sense. Are there some people who have found their soulmates?" I ask, but I already know the answer.

"Of course, I told you that Andrew and Gabby found each other. Andrews parents and yours—"

"My parents were soulmates?" I interrupt her.

"Yes." She glares, "Although more people don't find their soul-mates than do. And some do find them and don't work out." She explains. "Humans are weird. Love is...complicated." My mind drifts to thoughts of Zagreus.

I head out of the basement when Aph starts nodding off. I haven't gone to bed this early in a long time, but we have school tomorrow and it's her first day. Aph wanted to know what it felt like to be a normal human, so naturally she decided that she wanted to go try out high school. I haven't been going to school, I've ditched most of the new school year so far. The only reason I'm going tomorrow is because they've put me on academic probation and threatened to throw my dad in jail if I didn't start going again. It's not that I didn't like school, I mean it was something to do, but I know more about the world than any teacher could understand. Gods are real. Greek Mythology isn't myth. It's so real, it took my best friend away. How could anyone expect me to want to go back?

I'm visited by hellhounds in my dreams. They chase us to the edge of the Underworld, to the shores of the river Styx. Andrew pushes me out of the way, tells me to run and dives into the river. The hounds follow him in. Andrew breaches the top of the water, smiling in victory until his face begins to melt and I can see his bones. His eyes glow red and in a deep terrifying voice he yells at me. "Why did you leave me here? You left me behind to rot. You did this to me."

I wake up to the birds chirping away outside. I'm on the

floor, tangled in blankets and drenched in sweat. I left him there. *He told you to leave him.* That doesn't mean you had to. *They knocked you out, dragged you home.* I'll save him, I'll get him back somehow.

2

This is me trying

Gabby picks Aph and I up from my house around seven-thirty like Andrew used to do for me, even though she lives closer to the school and picking us up means that she is going out of her way. Aph grabs shotgun and I slide in the backseat.

"I grabbed coffee for you guys on the way here to celebrate Aph's first day!" Gabby chimes, she's starting to sound like her old self again. "Rose I got you a toasted white-hot chocolate with a shot of espresso, and Aph the vanilla frap with extra whip and caramel. Did I get it right?" She asks.

"Of course, thank you!" I tell her, Aph does the same. Gabby smiles brightly before pulling out of my driveway and heading to the school.

We park a few blocks away from the school so Gabby can smoke while we walk to campus. I'm not sure where she gets them or when she started smoking, but the extra few minutes outside is nice, even if it's clouded with cigarette smoke.

In the last four months, I've only been to school a handful of times. It's easy to ditch class when the student to teacher ratio is seventeen to one. I didn't go far when I ditched, I mostly spent my time hanging out in the forest behind the high school, but occasionally I'd venture out into town, going to coffee shops for the free WIFI or watching a movie at the theatre. I couldn't stand the looks people would give me at school. Even the teachers would look at me with sympathy or give me a little extra time on my homework. They didn't act like this when my mother died, and I didn't like all the extra attention. They didn't understand, my best friend wasn't dead. But to them he was, he was swept away by a flash flood, his body never recovered. If only they really *knew*.

Apparently, the school has made some arrangements to layout of the school since the last time I was here, and I walked into the wrong classroom three times before I figured out where my first hour was. Thankfully, Aph was also in my first hour, so we got lost together. All the annoyance on the teachers faces when I entered late, was wiped away the second they saw Aph. Our first class, economics, was taught by a middle-aged balding man, who seemed a little too excited to be welcoming Aph into the classroom. Aphrodite was used to having admirers though, and hardly noticed that he was checking her out as she walked to her assigned seat. I glared at him until he noticed before taking my own seat.

The same thing happened in science, while we were supposed to be dissecting frogs. Mr. Samuels also spent a disgusting amount of time around Aph. While she was getting sick from the smell, I was getting sick from the face he made when she bent over. When the bell rang for lunch, I grabbed her by the wrist and pulled her out of the room before we were even dismissed.

In the cafeteria, Gabby and Jess sit at the table that used to belong to Andrew and me. I place my tray on the table and pull out my seat.

"Hey guys!" Gabby smiles, she's oddly happy for once.

"Hey." I smile back.

"Did you guys hear the news?" Jessica asks.

"No, what happened?" Aph asks her.

"A bunch of people were found dead this morning. There were at least ten bodies taken in." Jess explains, her dad is a police officer so of course she would know that this wasn't on the news yet.

Gabby looks down at her spaghetti and pushes it away from her. "Actually, I don't think I'm that hungry anymore." She whispers to herself.

"What happened to them?" I ask Jess.

"Well, if you must know," She rolls her eyes at me, "At first, we thought it was a murderer on the loose, but none of the bodies had any injuries and some of them seemed to be in perfect health. So, we don't know yet." She explains. Aph gives me a knowing look that confuses me, but I figure I'll just ask her about it later. "I shouldn't be telling you all this though, so don't tell anyone." Jess spits.

"Like I have anyone to tell, Jessica." I roll my eyes and turn back to the cafeteria spaghetti in front of me but out of the corner of my eye I see Deme running out of the cafeteria, a group of girls laughing behind her. Two of the girls stand out from the pack and they look oddly similar aside from their differing hair colors, one has bright pastel blue hair, almost white, while the other has fiery red hair with black lowlights. They must be twins. They stand taller than most of the other girls, although one twin, the one with the blue hair, is shorter than the other.

"What's that about?" Gabby asks me.

"Not sure, but I'm gonna go find out." I tell her and I rush after my little sister.

I catch up to her in the girl's bathroom. She's in one of the stalls crying.

"Deme? What's going on?" I ask her though the door.

"Nothing, its fine. I'll be okay." She tells me.

"Okay, now tell me the truth." I say and she sniffles once more before opening the stall door for me.

"Wyatt and I broke up." She sniffles.

"Oh." I pull her into my arms and hug her tightly. "What happened?"

"I can't lie to myself anymore. Nix was right, I can't have a family if it means I'll die." She tells me, but something in the tone of her voice tells me that isn't the reason why she broke up with him.

"I'm sorry." I say and hug her tighter. "Is that why those girls were laughing?" I ask.

"No, I had another vision and fainted again."

"What did you see?" I ask her, wiping a tear from her cheek.

"Dead people." She chuckles though her tears, "Like that kid from that movie." She explains, and I can't help but laugh with her. I don't mention that the police found a bunch of dead people this morning, I don't want to scare her.

"Do you want to go home for the rest of the day, I can call dad to come check you out of school?" I ask but she shakes her head.

"No, I don't want to give them the satisfaction. But I'll call dad and let him know about the vision."

"Okay, sounds good to me. Who were those girls anyway, I didn't recognize them?"

"They're new, just moved here. Melanie and Mackenzie, or as I call them the wonder twins. Everyone seems to love them, just because they're new." She rolls her eyes. "But they're just a couple mean girls." She adds. The bell rings, signaling to us that our time is up.

"Are you sure that you're okay?" I ask. Deme nods so I hug her one more time before heading to home room.

I find it hard to focus the rest of the day. With everything that's been going on lately, I could really use a vacation. Deme is immortal, people are dying without cause, it's Aphrodite's first day of high school, don't even get me started on all the weird stares I get from everyone because the same month my best friend disappeared, my brother came home; But I fight the urge to ditch and stay at school the rest of the day.

As if this year couldn't get any worse, an announcement from the principal sends everyone into a panic, his nasally voice rings out from the intercoms.

"Attention students, as some of you may have heard, there have been many reports of deaths throughout our community today. While doctors and medical professionals are still not sure of the direct cause, the Center for Disease Control has placed

Paradise under a mandatory quarantine. This means that you will all be sent home for the foreseeable future; classes will continue online. Your parents and guardians have been notified of this and are on their way to come collect you. If you drove yourself to school, we are asking that you please be patient and wait until you are called to the parking lot. Please stay safe and remember, Go Longhorns!"

I look around at my classmates and notice their panicked faces, even our teacher looks terrified. I almost expect everyone to start running out into the hallways and start a riot, but everyone stays in their seats. I pull my phone out, along with everyone else and go straight to the news, but I can't find anything. Whatever is going on, no one even knows about it yet or they're too panicked to write any articles about it.

"If the CDC is here, then that means something really bad must have happened to those dead people." One kid, Michael whispers to someone.

"Maybe they have the Black Plague! I heard it was found on some opossums down in Flagstaff!" Another kid says.

"It's been like hundreds of years, dude. There's a cure for the Black Plague now." Someone answers.

"Maybe its zombies, like in that one show! That would be sick!"

"Really? *Zombies?*"

"Well, it's better than Black Plague."

I listen to the group next to me theorize over many different possibilities as to why the CDC is here, but none of them are even remotely interesting. They get stuck on the zombie thing for almost twenty minutes. Eventually the room thins out.

Students leave one after the other when their names are called on the intercoms in the classrooms.

"Phoenix, Demeter, and Rose Knight along with Daphne Onassis, please make your way to the pickup area, your guardian is here to take you home." The office secretary calls over the intercom. I pack my stuff up and head to the main office, where I find my siblings and Aph. Aph gives me a funny look but doesn't say anything as we make our way to the pickup location. Dad is waiting in the car, he traded in his truck for an old green Jeep Wagoneer from the seventies a couple months ago so we'd have a vehicle all of us would fit in until we could get another car for us kids to use. It was old, looked like a tank and most of the seats had holes in them, but it got the job done and Dad was always a sucker for the classics.

Nix slides in the front while us girls slide into the back-seat and squish together; Dad doesn't say a word until we get on the road. He looks angry but scared at the same time if that's even possible.

"Do you kids know anything about what's going on?" He asks.

"Jessica mentioned something about a bunch of dead bodies being found this morning, but that's all I heard." I tell him.

"All the kids at school think its some sort of disease, since the CDC is shutting the town down." Nix says. Dad ponders this for a moment as I'm reminded of something that Areon told me a long time ago.

"Yeah well, they also think its zombies, so..." Deme chimes in.

"Hades did something like this." I blurt, everyone turns to look at me, but they don't say anything. "Areon told me that Hades used the Bubonic Plague as a cover up to build an Army of the Dead. Re-animating the corpses and such. I didn't really go into much detail with him about it though." I explain.

"Aphrodite?" My dad raises his eyebrows and looks at her in the rear-view mirror.

"She's right." Aphrodite tells him, "The Black Plague was another way that Hades attempted to expose us to the world. It's one of his favorite things to do, play tricks on us, start wars for no reason, anything to annoy his brothers. He drove Ares mad with all the wars he has almost started. But being here with you guys I'm out of the loop." She explains, but I get the feeling she's hiding something. She's avoiding eye contact with everyone, and her leg is bouncing up in down.

"Well, we'll need to be very careful regardless of if this is a disease or not." Dad tells us. "The whole town is pretty much shut down; the stores are only open for grocery pickup and my job has been put on hold until all of this is over. Hopefully, we pass through this quietly and it doesn't spread. The last thing we need is a pandemic." I look outside, sure enough, in the parking lots of the grocery stores people are panicking. Carts are being pushed hastily into their place; grocery bags thrown carelessly into the backs of people's cars. The gas stations are packed as well, each gas pump backed up at least three cars, people coming in and out of the store carrying packs of water and soda. Traffic is more backed up than usual as well, normally we don't get so backed up on the weekdays unless it's snowing, and the tourists are in town.

3

Darkside

Time passed slowly in this seemingly endless quarantine.

The remaining leaves on the ground withered, as the cold came and coated the entire town with a thick blanket of snow. Thanksgiving came and went, the first holiday we spent with Aph, who put away more food than I've ever seen Andrew eat in one sitting. More people passed away; I think the total number is somewhere close to one hundred. Classes were cancelled for the remainder of the year, but we still have to do these packets that the school mailed out.

Dad was working again, he's in charge of building a new set of community homes with a small work crew, but this wasn't the case for everyone. Most of the businesses in town closed, many of them for good, sport events and musicals were all cancelled too.

Being home this much was a challenge for all of us. Although I had an easier time than my siblings and Aph, I liked being shut up in my room. Headphones were all I needed to get through the day. It's not like I slept anyway but sleeping seemed easier when I wasn't forced to be aware of what time of day it was or even what day of the week it was. My nights blended into days and my hours turned into weeks.

I lay in bed listening to loud music to distract myself from how badly I want to be outside, it works for a little bit. Doors slam open and shut so much that I'm forced to pull my headphones off and get off my bed to look out the window. Dads' jeep is parked out front and he run back and forth, in and out of the house to the vehicle. I watch him for a minute as he stops, pulls a small bottle from his jacket pocket, chugs it, then pulls out his phone. I hear him yelling but can't quite understand what he is saying through the thick glass. Something bad must've happened. I head out into the hall to go see what's happening, but Deme stops me before I reach the stairs.

"Don't." She warns, I give her a puzzled look. "One of his crew members died."

"How do you—" I stop, I already know how she knows. She had another vision. I can tell by the dark circles under her eyes.

"He's on the phone with the police right now." She tells me, Nix has come out of his room now, his golden locks hang messily around his ears.

"What's going on?" He asks sleepily.

"Bill is dead." Deme says, he searches his brain for a Bill before it clicks, and he looks sad. "But that's not all." She almost whispers, and she suddenly looks sick.

"Well spit it out already." Nix rubs the back of his head. He needs a haircut, badly. His blonde mop is rolled on the top of his head in a bun.

"It isn't a disease that's killing these people. It's a monster." She shudders at the thought.

A monster?

What does that even mean?

I don't get a chance to think about it much though because a second later Dad is slamming the door and calling us all into living room, including Aph.

I'm not sure how to feel. What kind of monster could kill people and make it look like a disease was doing it? Is this like the black plague again? Is Hades planning another coup? I sit across from Deme on the floor, Aph and Nix have taken up residence on the couch while dad paces the floor in front of us. I try to make eye contact with Deme, maybe she can whisper what it is to me. But before I can try, Dad interrupts me.

"They're back." He says to Aphrodite, making serious eye contact with her. The way his face contorts reminds me of Jack Nicholson in The Shining. *Here's Johnny!*

"What are you talking about? What's back?" She's playing dumb, I can tell by the tone in her voice. Its higher than it usually is. She twirls a golden lock of hair around her finger.

"You know damn well what I'm talking about." He tells her, "How long have you known? Why didn't you say anything?" He demands.

"Dad—" I start but I get cut off again.

"Stay out of this!" He yells and I can feel myself shrink further towards the floor. Deme grabs my hand and squeezes it tightly.

"I didn't know, okay. Not until it was already too late." Aphrodite defends herself.

"Too late yeah?" He scoffs, "So I suppose you just thought it was safer to not say anything at all then? To wait until half the town was dead."

"I didn't—."

"What the hell is going on?" I yell, feeling suddenly braver. Dad turns his annoyance to me.

"Nothing much, just that one of the most powerful creatures is making its way around town, killing everyone that we love. And she—" He turns back to Aph, "knew exactly what it was, right from the beginning."

"You can't stop them, you know that! This town was already doomed." Aphrodite yells, her voice carries around the room unexpectedly and I'm reminded that she is a powerful Goddess, she probably hasn't been talked to like this in her entire existence.

"What are they?" I ask and everyone stops, Dads pacing ends and he won't make eye contact with me, neither will Aph. "Seriously, someone better tell me before I go find out for myself." I warn.

"They're called Vrykolakas." Aph says quietly.

"Vry-cola-what?" Nix asks.

"Vrykolakas," Dad says again, "Most call them The Vry."

"Okay, but what are they?" I ask.

"Vampires." Dad spits.

You have got to be kidding me.

Vampires. Really?

"They aren't Vampires," Aph laughs, "far from it. Although, they do share some similar qualities with the vampires from those movies you watch. But they do not bite, they spread death with disease." She explains. So, it *technically* is a disease. "They also don't hunger for blood, they rarely eat, but if they do, they prefer the liver." I gag at the thought.

"Can they be killed?" Nix asks.

Aphrodite laughs again, "If you can get close enough, yes. But good luck. They're already dead, the only way to truly kill them is with a stake to the heart if you can get close enough without it scratching your eyes out with its nasty fingernails." She shudders. "Talk about needing a manicure." She sounds exactly like she had when I first met her. Conceded, arrogant, vain. I *definitely* didn't miss this version of her.

"So how can it be too late? If they can be killed, then let's go kill them." Nix says and this time, its dad who laughs.

"You just got back from the Underworld boy, and you're ready to go back that quickly?" He starts pacing again, "Going after them is a death wish." I'm getting a headache and I'm suddenly aware of how sweaty my palm is getting in Deme's hand.

"How do you know it's the Vry?" I ask, wiping my hand on my jeans.

"You sister saw them and described them to me." Dad points at Deme.

"And what do they look like?" Nix asks, everyone looks at Deme.

"Zombies, basically. Only their bodies are almost swollen and elongated." Deme explains. She sounds tired.

"So, these zombie-vampires are just running around the town killing everyone with a scratch?" Nix shakes his head, "Wouldn't more people be dead?" He asks.

"No, not necessarily, they have rules, and it isn't through scratching. They can't kill you if you don't answer them unless you attack first. Although it's a challenge not to answer them. A normal person would open the door before they even realized there was something wrong, by then it's too late." Dad says, he finally sits down in his recliner across from the couch. I relax a little with him.

"Answer the door?" Nix looks confused, "What? They just knock on the door and say I'm here to kill you?" He says this mockingly.

"Yes, they knock on your door, sometimes they even call out your name. They can mimic anyone, a dead loved one, a long lost parent or sibling, and if you answer, you die. If not, you live. They will only knock once. If the dead are not buried on sacred ground, they will also become a member of the Vrykolakas in a few days." Aphrodite explains.

"So those people that the CDC are testing on, they'll—" I start.

"They'll most likely become one if they aren't put to rest in time, yes." Dad answers.

"So, let's kill them before they kill more of us." Nix states again.

"I refuse to risk losing any of you to them" Dad tells us, although he glances at Aph like she's the exception to his statement.

"What about Zagreus then?" Nix says, Aph and Deme look straight at me. I can feel my face flush of all its color.

"What about him?" I hear myself saying, a pit develops in my stomach.

"What do you mean? He's literally the hunter of the

underworld, shouldn't he be here killing them or something?" Nix says. Heat begins to rise in my cheeks.

"Not if Hades is the one sending them." Aph states.

I want to throw up.

The sun sets on us before we have come to an agreement. As it stands now, Aphrodite can't interfere, because *of course* she can't. Nix wants to go in guns blazing, like we're some sort of superhero team. Deme doesn't want to do anything. And Dad, is somewhere in the middle. I don't care what we do, as long as Zagreus isn't involved. I mean it's not like I even know how to get ahold of him if I wanted to, but still.

I get up midway through a conversation, only to get a dirty look from Dad.

"Where—?"

"Pizza," I cut him off, "I'm starving and didn't eat lunch." I head into the kitchen and order three pizzas, sausage, supreme, and cheese. Ordering takeout has become the only source of business most places can count on and even then, they have to leave the order at the door. Deme joins me in the kitchen after I hang up the phone, sitting down at the table across from me. She hasn't said much all day, the visions are taking too much out of her.

"Rose, Can I ask you something?" She says, I nod in response. "Why don't you want to involve Areon? What did he do?" She asks. I frown, I never told her what happened. I never told anyone what happened between us, the night we destroyed Andrew's truck, the fight between us. No one needed to know. I didn't want to relive it.

"We got into a fight." I tell her.

"About what?" She asks curiously. I look down at the worn wood of the kitchen table and then up at the ceiling. A hint of glitter catches my eye. It's puffy paint, still stuck to the roof after all these years. Deme and I had been making something when the bottle refused to let anymore paint escape from the tube, we squeezed it so hard that it came rocketing out and onto the ceiling. It's amazing how long its lasted up there, I'm not sure anyone else would even notice it unless they were looking for it. "Rose, you can tell me." Deme says.

"He wanted to erase my memories." I sigh, Deme looks visibly shocked.

"Wait, what?" She asks.

"Not all of them, just of everything that had happened. He'd make me forget leaving Andrew behind, forget that he even went down with us at all." I explain.

"Rose, maybe he was just—"

"Don't try to justify it, Deme. He wanted to erase my memories after years of me trying to get them back. He wanted me to forget my best friend, forget what I did to him. I couldn't..." I trail off, tears fill my eyes. Deme reaches out and grabs my hands in hers.

"Rose, maybe he was just trying to help you in one of the only ways he knew how? Maybe he just didn't want to see you hurting as bad as you were." She tells me, squeezing my hands.

"He came to see me again after that. At Andrews funeral." I tell her.

"What happened?"

"Nothing. I wouldn't talk to him. I wouldn't even let him get a word out. I told him to go away, and that I never wanted to see him again." I say quietly.

"Rose." She sighs and closes her eyes.

"What?"

"You need to learn to control your emotions better. You let them get the best of you too often." Deme tells me. When did she get so old? When did she become so much wiser and smarter? It feels like yesterday she was sitting on the ground surrounded by a battlefield of Barbies and stuffed animals. I squeeze her hands this time.

"I know." I breathe back the tears, "I just can't help it." I tell her.

A knock at the door makes us jump, Deme and I look at each other silently, everyone in the other room quiets down as well. I'd almost forgotten that we were in the middle of a Vampire-Zombie Pandemic. Nobody says anything for a minute. Another knock puts us at ease.

"Pizza!" A voice calls out. "I'll just leave the order on the porch." It sounds like a teenager not much older than me or Deme. Dad is the first to start for the door, but he waits another five minutes before looking out the window.

"Come on Dad, the pizza is getting cold!" Nix calls out, Deme and I giggle. Dad opens the door and brings three pizza boxes into the kitchen.

I wake up on the couch around sunrise with a blanket draped over me. Bright oranges and pinks illuminate the room around me through the wide window in the living room. I have no idea when I fell asleep, but the conversation droned on for hours after we finished dinner and we still haven't decided what we are going to do. I listen to the world around me. Birds chirp happily outside of the windows, squirrels run along the telephone wires, the hum of a car as it warms up in some one's driveway, I can hear it all. The house is quiet, although I think I can hear a snore from downstairs, it's difficult to make out through the thick layers of cement. I never thought Aphrodite would have a flaw, I never would have guessed it was snoring.

This would be the perfect time to sneak out. No one would notice, and I'd even get a couple of hours to myself. I quietly make my way upstairs to grab some shoes and head out the door as quickly as I can.

The sun warms my cheeks, but it is still cold enough outside to see my breath. I walk as quietly as I can to the edge of the driveway and across the street. Dad got to keep some of the perks of being a wolf after he gave up the ability to transform, so I'm hoping that he's so deep asleep that he can't hear my footsteps. Once I reach the edge of the forest, I take off running. I run until my fingers are red and tingle from the cold, and I keep running after. Until I'm lost in the woods, until I am only a wolf in the forest. Fur and fangs, trees, and unknown lands. I run until I'm not me anymore because when I'm a wolf, I don't have to feel anything. Not afraid, not sad, not desperate, or guilty. Nothing at all.

I stand at the top of a cliff; the same one Areon took me to the very first day we spent together. It overlooks the entire city of Paradise; you can see everything from here. The coffee shop I used to work at, the movie theater, the school, the grocery stores, football fields, everything. Our tiny, sleepy, snow-covered little town nestled in a valley of pine trees. The snow glistens off the buildings and trees as the rays of the morning sun, shine down. I used to wonder what would bring anyone here. Maybe for a cool vacation yeah, but to live here? I used to think people were crazy for living here or for leaving and coming back. Now, I look at the town with some sort of nostalgia. I miss the smell of the woods before the snow killed all the plants and I long for the summer nights out by the rivers. Paradise is beautiful and the perfect place to settle down, raise kids, and retire. The American dream of white picket fences and a tight knit community is strong here. That doesn't mean that the town doesn't have its faults. There isn't much for kids and teens to do, so there's a decent amount of graffiti and vandalism in the parks where teens do hang out.

And there are *a lot* of parties.

I haven't thought about the party in a long time. The one where Tyler tried to hurt me, where Areon defended me. I blocked most of the night out, being intoxicated helped block those memories too, but I still have nightmares of Tyler. Sometimes I can still feel his hand around my neck, the oxygen leaving my body. I shiver in the breeze. Tyler was arrested and I can defend myself now. I don't have to worry about him anymore. His case was basically open and shut, once the first girl came forward, more and more came forward with their own stories. They tried him as an adult and sent him to prison, I don't remember how long he's there for. Once he'd been found guilty, I shut everything else out.

The sun has risen in the sky, I've probably been out here for an hour at least. Cars are moving throughout town now, but not as many as I'd once seen. The "quarantine" has the entire town scared and nobody can leave until they figure out what it is that's causing the disease. If only the CDC *really* knew what was going on, they'd lose their minds.

I should head home soon but being out here is nice. I'd almost forgotten what fresh air felt like. The others might be up by now though and I'd rather not worry them.

"Rose."

I freeze at the voice behind me. His smooth voice almost chills me to the bone, and I feel paralyzed. No. He can't be here. *He can't be here.* I wasn't prepared to see him again. I slowly turn to face him, only to find that nobody is there. I look everywhere but I can't see him. But I'd heard him. Am I going insane? Areon was here. His voice was right behind me. He couldn't have disappeared that quickly, could he? Who am I kidding? Yes, he can. He uses portals to travel, of course he could disappear that quickly. I take a deep breath and turn my back on the town, I need to get home.

I arrive at home, just in time to get yelled at by my dad for leaving in the first place.

"But dad, it's light out. I was perfectly safe."

"You didn't even leave a note, never mind that its light out. You could have been taken last night and we'd never known." He sighs, "I'm glad you're safe, but you still snuck out. Go to your room." He commands me. I obey and turn to the stairs. I think about telling him about Areon, but I shake my head and make my way upstairs without another word.

The shower feels nice, I can't remember the last time I got to it before Nix or Deme. I actually got the hot water for once. Although it isn't long until Nix is pounding on the door telling me to get out. I turn off the tap and step out into the cold winter air. I wrap a towel around myself and wipe the condensation off the mirror. My blond hair sticks to my skin, and I'm a lot skinnier than I'd like to be, but the sleep I've been getting lately makes my skin glow. It's almost as if the universe knew how tired I've been and finally gave me a break from the nightmares.

I pass Nix in the hallway, and he doesn't make a sound as he slips into the bathroom after me, locking the door behind him. I hurry into my room and shut the door to get dressed. I haven't done laundry in a while, so I'm stuck wearing my moms old Fleetwood Mac tee I've kept and a pair of over-worn ripped jeans.

Downstairs, the house smells like bacon, eggs, and sausage. The only breakfast foods my dad knows how to cook. But I can smell something else, something metallic I think, although I can't quite put a name to it with all the other smells mixed in. My senses have been heightened but I'm still learning to use them, especially smell. By the time we were all finished with breakfast the overwhelming smells of the food had dissipated and it finally hit me what that foreign scent was. But by now I know it's too late. I run to the window and stare out at the neighbors across the street. Sure enough, an ambulance is sitting on the curb. Dad and Nix join me before Dad walks out onto the porch to get a closer look and see what's happened.

A body bag on a stretcher is rolled out of the house, and even across the street and behind the walls of my own house, my nose is filled with the sickly smell of a dead body. A man walks out of the house behind the paramedics, clearly the husband, he has tears pouring down his face and isn't even trying to hide them. I watch as they begin to transfer the stretcher to the back of the ambulance. A child runs out of the house, she's small, no older than five, and she's holding a teddy bear. I can't make out what she is saying, mostly because it doesn't even sound like real words, but her blonde hair flaps in the winter wind behind her as she runs up to the stretcher and tucks her teddy bear into one of the straps. Her father rushes to pick her up and seems to be crying even harder, he's almost hysterical at this point but he holds onto his daughter tightly. I'm not even sure she knows what is happening.

A little girl lost her mother.

She will grow up without her. She won't be there for her first date, or her first kiss, or to see her graduate school or get married. Because of the Vry. Because of these monsters, she will grow up without that support system. Just like me and Deme and Nix.

Life isn't fair.

Phoenix is right. We need to do something; *I* need to do something. The Vry need to be stopped. I can't just sit back and let this happen to people. I cannot let them destroy people's lives.

There must be something that I can do.

I excuse myself and head upstairs to my room, locking the door behind me. I'm leaving, I've already made that decision, and no one is coming with me. I grab an old bag from the back of my closet and realize there are still clothes in it from the last time I left. When we went to the Underworld. Torn clothes that I never dealt with, now stained and crusty from blood. I throw them in the trash next to my desk and dump the crumbs at the bottom of the bag into it too. I start packing, with a blanket on the bottom, then stuff some warmer clothes in, sweatpants and hoodies, a small pillow, a flashlight and batteries, some granola bars I had stuffed in my desk, and a lighter. I stare at my phone, I shouldn't bring it, it'll only be a distraction and Deme won't stop calling. I put the phone into the drawer of my bedside table. I look around the room, one last look to see if there is anything I've forgotten.

After dinner I excused myself to my room. Nix had done the same while Dad and Deme went to the living room to watch TV. I quietly place my bag outside my window on the roof, I wait and listen. Downstairs, the television booms with sound, louder than it needs to be, which is perfect. I step out onto the roof and get hit with the cold winter air. I breathe it in, better to get used to it now. Who knows how long I'll be out here hunting these things? I won't be back until all of them are dead, or until I'm brought home in a body bag. I silently close the window, although there is no way to lock it from the outside, so I hope it doesn't blow open in the middle of the night. I grab my bag and make my way to the edge of the roof. My window is above the living room, but if I walk to the left corner, I should be hidden from the view of the window.

I hit the wet dirt with a quiet thud and make my way to the property line before I start running. Once I do, I take off in the direction of the old, abandoned house that served as my childhood fort. I turn into a wolf, but I can still feel the backpack sitting on my spine. It bounces along with me as I navigate my way through the woods. I wasn't sure what happened to my clothes when I transformed, I always assumed they just got absorbed into my body somehow, apparently this magic doesn't work on my backpack though. If there were any game cameras out here, some hunter was going to get a show.

The fort is waiting for me just like it always is. I light a few candles with the lighter I brought and spread out the blanket and pillow on the floorboards. It feels cold enough to snow, but I have a job to do. I can't let a little cold weather hold me back, and even if it does snow, it'll help. Snow covers scents and if I manage to get a hint of what these things smell like, I should have an easier time differentiating it from every other track that's out there. I might have to stay in my wolf form if it gets too cold though, I'm not sure if I should risk starting a fire in the decaying fireplace, I might end up setting the whole building on fire.

A twig snaps outside and I freeze. I hear nothing else, so I peek my head out of the doorway. I can't see anything or smell anything. It must've been the wind or a pinecone falling from a tree. I settle back into my little nest and pull out a granola bar. When we were children, our mom used to tell us, *"They say there is a mountain lion within one-hundred feet of you at all times, living out here."* Although I never really believed her, and she never said who "They" were. I've never even seen a mountain lion before that wasn't in a zoo. Maybe a better term would be a predator. It doesn't matter where you live, there is always a predator lurking somewhere close, whether it's a mountain lion, a creepy man in the shadows of your city, or a teenage boy at a party in the middle of nowhere. But not tonight.

Tonight, *I* am the predator.

4

Weapon

I catch the scent of the Vry all over the house across the street from mine, although it is very faint now. They moved faster than I thought they would; I never would have thought that rotting corpses could move any faster than the zombies I see in the movies. The family still hasn't come home. The house is dark, and the curtains are all still open. It's a dark contrast to my own brightly lit home across the street. The front porch light glares at me, daring me to come back to the safety of its walls, but I can't. If I go home now, more people will die. I can't let that happen. A bright light powers on above me and I stop, frozen in my spot. It's a security light though, not a soul around.

Even if anyone was around, I don't know what I'm so worried for. I came here as wolf for just that reason. I knew if someone saw a girl lurking outside a house the cops may have been called because they saw an "intruder". Which, they wouldn't be completely wrong. Being a wolf is much safer for this for more reasons than I can count, plus, my tracking skills are much better when I'm transformed and to any onlookers, I'm just a stray carrying a stick in its mouth.

I carved a stake from a fallen branch back at the fort. I'm not sure if I did it right, and I have more splinters than I'd like to admit, but I think I did a surprisingly good job. Hopefully, the stake didn't need to be carved from a specific type of wood and I'll be fine. But carrying it around in my mouth is becoming more and more annoying by the minute. I'm going to need to put it down soon. I skulk around the block, following the scent along the sidewalk. How these things can move around in plain sight is beyond me. They smell exactly like I thought they might, rotting corpses. They smell remarkably close to the way Areons' body had smelled when I found it as a child all those years ago. I'd forgotten how it smelled until I found this scent. The Vry are more putrid though, like they've been baking in an oven for weeks.

A raindrop hits my nose and I break into a run.

If I don't hurry, the rain will wash away the trail and I will be back to the drawing board. I need to find them. I need to end this. The track stays on the sidewalk, heading away from the forest and heading towards town. Where more innocent people could be killed. Where Gabby is at risk of being killed. I'd never thought about Gabby being a risk before. But she would definitely answer the door if they managed to mimic Andrew's voice. She'd answer it in a heartbeat.

A different scent hits my nose. It is familiar too. There's a hint of cinnamon, maybe vanilla too.

I realize too late that I'm smelling a human.

I turn a corner and smash face first into the chest of a man. We collide so hard he's thrown backward, and the stake flies out of my mouth and thuds loudly against the asphalt in the middle of the street. I scramble away from the human and towards the stake. I need to hurry now. The raindrops are starting to fall even heavier now. Puddles are starting to form in the street.

"Rose?"

Oh no.

No. *No.*

Not now.

Hell no.

I turn back toward the human and sure enough, still sitting on the sidewalk, recovering from our collision, with his perfectly chiseled God-like face, is Zagreus.

I don't have time for this. I don't have time for his games and lies. There are people in danger. People I care about who are in danger. I lunge for the stake, grabbing it with my mouth and shake myself off before I take off back down the street. I merge with the scent of the Vry again on the sidewalk, but now it is tainted. I can smell Zagreus more than I can them and its distracting.

I've been running around town aimlessly for hours. I lost the Vry miles ago and now I'm just trying to force Zagreus out of my head. I turn down a random street, one I've never been on before and slow down. Why is he here? Why now? Is he controlling the Vry? No. He was going in the opposite direction of me. If he was leading them, wouldn't they be with him? Then why is he here? Did they escape the Underworld and now he's hunting them? That would explain the weapons he had strapped to his back. How did he even recognize me? There are wolves in the area. Nix is a wolf, why not assume it was him? *Because Nix can't turn into a full wolf.* But there are wild wolves in the area too, why not assume it was one of them? *What kind of wolf would be carrying a stake in its mouth?*

I stop walking.

There aren't any lights on in this area. The streetlamps are all out and not even a porch light is on. The street is pitch black. If I were a human, I wouldn't be able to see a foot in front of me. The rain is lightly falling from the sky, and I try to smell the area around me.

They're here.

I can't see them, but I can faintly make out the scent of them. The Vry are somewhere on this street.

I search the street, going from house to house. I clear them one by one, making sure to search the yards before moving on to the next one. The scent grows stronger as I move down the street. All I can hope for is that they haven't found a target before I can get to them.

I find the Vry a few houses down. The putrid smell overwhelms my nose, but I force myself closer and sure enough, three of them are moving at a crawl towards the only house on the street that has lights on. They are truly, the most disgusting creatures I have ever laid my eyes on. They are human-like, only distended with a ruddy complexion. Like they've been bathing in blood and soaking it into their bodies like a sponge. Peculiarly, as they get closer to the lights of the house, they don't have shadows; like they aren't even there at all. I can't help but want to get closer to them, but I don't move from the shadows. They don't know I'm here and I'm not ready to show them.

I didn't actually come up with a plan.

I mean I carved a stake, but only one, and what if I have to leave the stake in its heart in order to actually kill it. I hadn't thought ahead at all. I hear three knocks and look back to the house. One of the Vry has reached the door, the other two are standing back a bit, frozen in place as they wait. Other than knocking they haven't made any other sounds. But their attention is on the door. Now is my chance, I only have a few moments before they'll move on to the next house if these people decide not to answer the door. And if they do answer the door, it'll be too late for me to save them. Zagreus had weapons. He had a spear, arrows. Maybe it doesn't matter what you impale them with, as long as it's something sharp and goes through the heart.

How am I supposed to impale them when I don't have thumbs?

I'm running out of time. I can almost hear the time running down in my head. *Tick-tock, tick-tock.*

I lunge towards the creatures, waiting until the last second to turn back into a human. I grab the stake from my mouth mid transformation and plunge it deep into the back of one of the creatures, I can feel its bones scraping against the splintered wood in my hands as I thrust it deeper into the creature. I hope I calculated where its heart would be right, but the closer I got, the more disfigured the creature looked, and it was hard to tell. The beast cries out. An ear-splitting sound that knocks me off balance and before I know it, the other two Vry are next to the one I impaled and looking for the source of the attack. I take this distraction to my advantage and turn back into a wolf. I frantically look around for something else I can use against them. The house itself is the only wooden object in my vicinity and I have no choice but to try to pry a small beam on the deck fencing from its housing to use as a weapon. I take hold of the wooden bar in my mouth and pull as hard as I can, but the Vry beat me to it. I'm thrown to the grass in front of the house and the wind gets knocked out of me.

They don't even give me a second to recover before they're on me again.

Long nails dig deep into my side before I roll away and get to my feet. The rusty smell of my own blood makes me a little dizzy, but I force the feeling away and jump for one of the monsters. I grab its arm and pull, ripping it from its socket and shaking it vigorously before the beast launches me away from it. I land on all fours on the porch, scraping the deck with my claws as I catch my balance. I go for the wooden beams again; I'd done a number on it before the Vry had ripped me from it and find it relatively easy to pull it from the rest of the fence.

With my new weapon, I circle around them. The one I'd already staked is still moving, but barely. There is no doubt in my mind that if I had pulled it out, the monster would have been up and fighting already. The other two are keeping pace with me easily, easier than I'd like to admit. I'd had a strong advantage by catching them off guard. I'm going to have a really hard time fighting the two of them while injured. I'm going to have to try to separate them somehow if I'm going to live through this.

I run to the back yard, fully aware of the blood trail I am now leaving all over these stranger's yard. I'm not sure how much longer I'm going to be able to fight like this. In the shadows, I hide behind a tree that is holding a small treehouse on the top of it. I grab one of the wooden steps nailed lazily into the trunk of the tree and pull it out with the nails still in it. Now that I have a second weapon, and maybe even more, I'm not so afraid of losing the first one. I transform back into a human, the amount of pain I feel during the transformation is alarming. I'm hurt more than I thought I was. I sneak a peek at the claw marks from the Vry. My shirt is soaked in coagulated blood, thick and mucus-like, but I ignore my urge to vomit and pull up my shirt. The wound is turning black, like its infected. Black spiderweb-like lines travel from the wound to the rest of my side. The infection is spreading. I shove my shirt back down and turn my attention back to the surrounding Vry.

These things are quiet, I can't believe how silent their movements are, especially on the grass. Although, I did take some hearing loss by changing back into a human. I'm not even sure if I can change back into a wolf fast enough at this point without sustaining another injury from one of them. I have the beam from the porch and a plank of wood with a few nails in it that would do a decent amount of damage to one of them if I can move fast enough, but I can't trust my adrenaline anymore. My vision is blurring, and I feel wobbly just standing still.

A sharp whistle flies past me so quickly I can't follow the

sound. One of the Vry cries out in its high-pitched squeal again and I risk a peek at what is going on.

Of course, he would follow me.

I roll my eyes. An arrow is sticking out from the chest of one of the Vry and it falls to the ground. I don't hesitate. While the remaining Vry is distracted by the others cry of pain, I jump out from behind the tree and hit it as hard as I can in the head with the plank of wood. The nails stick into the side of its head. I let go of the plank and grab the beam from the ground next to me and shove it into its swollen chest, ignoring the sickening sounds of its lungs filling with fluid. I push down into the creature with every ounce of strength I can muster. Bone's crack and move out of the way as I push the weapon more than halfway through the Vry's body. The high-pitched scream fills my ears. I can't tell if the monster is still screaming or if my ears are just ringing while I plunge the remainder of the beam deep into its body, finally I collapse in exhaustion next to its still squirming corpse.

Rain blurs my sight as the dark clouds above me begin to pour out again. I turn my head and make out the body of the Vry next to me. It has stopped moving, and if I'm not mistaken, has started disintegrating into the ground before my eyes. I look back at the house, the lights are still on. These people are either the heaviest sleepers or are the only people in town smart enough to mind their own business. A squishy sound makes its way towards me, and Zagreus bends over, looking down at me.

"Rose, are you okay?" He asks.

I cough, "Hurt." I muster, "Infection." I reach for the hem of my shirt and begin pulling it up. Zagreus turns his attention to my wound.

"It's healing. You'll be fine. Are there anymore?" He asks. I shake my head. He leaves my side, I can't see him, but I can hear his footsteps squishing in the wet grass as he walks around the yard. The Vry that was next to me is now a big puddle of blood, the wooden beam now laying on the grass, I watch as the rain slowly washes it clean.

I wake up in a bundle of blankets on the floor of the fort, drenched in sweat and covered in my own dried blood. The sun shines through the cracks in the ceiling, water leftover from the rain drips in with it. I sit up and pull the blankets off me. I pull my shirt up over my head and observe my wound. The spider-webbing is gone but there are four long scars where the Vry had scratched me; they aren't healing anymore.

"That could have killed you." Zagreus says, I let out a shriek and pull the blankets up to cover my chest, realizing I'm only in my bra. His hair is cut short now, and he's wearing dark clothes under a metal breastplate. I stare at him; he looks older some-how. Even though I know that he doesn't age. I guess if Aph can change her appearance, He must be able to as well.

"What are you doing here?" I ask him.

"Better question, *what the hell* do you think you're doing hunting the Vrykolakas on your own?"

"I don't have to answer to you."

"Neither do I." He states and raises an eyebrow. We stare at each other for a few minutes, neither of us backing down until he shrugs. "I'm doing my Job, I'm hunting. Your turn."

"I needed to kill them before they killed anyone else."

"You nearly got yourself killed in the process, what made you think you could take them on? You know literally nothing about them." He tells me.

"I know more than you think I do." I state.

"Did you know that you would have died from those scratches if the one who did it, hadn't been killed first?" He asks, I don't answer. "Didn't think so. Where is your family? Why are you by yourself?"

"I didn't want them to get hurt."

"Rose, you need to get that hero-complex checked. You can't save everyone." He tells me. "What good would you have been if you died? You couldn't have saved them then."

"I don't have a hero-complex."

"No? Then what are you doing?" He asks.

I roll my eyes, "You're the one with the hero-complex, you keep showing up to save me when I don't need you."

"I wouldn't need to save you if you didn't keep putting yourself in harms way. Did you learn nothing from your run in with the chimera?" He's angrier than I've ever seen him, and I feel small. Childlike.

"Why are you here? I don't want you to be, just go away."

"I don't have a choice, Rose."

"I'll take care of the Vry, just go."

"Oh, you'll take care of them? Rose, we're talking in circles. You are going to die if you don't stop chasing them. Is that what you want? To die?" He spits.

"Maybe." I whisper.

"Excuse me?" He gets close to me, all the anger wiped from his face.

"I said maybe. Maybe being here is too hard. Continuing to

live while Andrew is stuck down there. Making friends, going to high school. None of it feels worth it anymore. It should have been me. I should have been the one left behind, not Andrew. He had a family that loves him, friends that love him, and a soulmate that misses him." I sigh, "Where is he? Why can't you help me bring him back?" I ask, tears spill from my eyes.

"I don't know where he is." He tells me, slouching against the framing of the fort.

"How, you literally live down there?" I ask.

"Because they won't let me see him. I've been stuck hunting monster after monster, day after day as a punishment for aiding the escape of the wolves. I can't help you because I don't even know where to start helping."

"I—wait, I don't understand. You haven't been in the underworld? You don't know where he is? How is that possible. Monsters don't just escape from the underworld, you said so yourself."

"They aren't escaping, they are being released in order to keep me busy." He sighs, "I haven't seen Andrew since the day we left him behind. I don't know where he is being kept, I don't know if he is still alive. I don't know what they are planning."

"Why would they do that?" I ask.

"I can only assume. I believe they are using the Vrykolakas to create an undead army like they did back during the Black Plague. I wouldn't have been onto them if I wasn't so good at hunting. I'd captured each creature my parents released and heard about the town going under quarantine from Hermes and decided to check it out for myself."

"Hermes?"

"Yeah, he works as a messenger for the Gods, so he spends a great deal of time traveling around the world and observing. If Hermes knows any more than just your town being shut down from a sickness, you guys really are in trouble. Zeus will destroy this town without blinking in order to keep the Gods a secret. Of course, that wouldn't stop my parents from sending the Vrykolakas to another city or town. Zeus would just be delaying the inevitable. I suspect the only reason they started with Paradise was to take you down and teach me a lesson." He explains.

"I—," I start, but I don't know what to say.

"Once I realized the Vrykolakas were behind this, I knew I had to come stop them. I didn't think I would even see you until we literally ran into each other on the street last night." He continues.

"How did you know it was me?" I ask.

"How many wolves carry wooden stakes around in the middle town that you know of?" He asks sarcastically.

"But it could have been another wolf, why me?"

"Rose, your family are the only ones in the area, and you are the only one who can shift into a full wolf." He rolls his eyes, "Now tell me why you're alone."

"I wasn't lying, I didn't want them to get hurt."

"They have no idea that you left, do they?" He asks, I don't answer. "Of course, they don't. Phoenix never would have let you go without him. He's too headstrong to have let you."

"If you're not going to leave, can you at least turn around so I can put a shirt on?" I ask, suddenly aware of how exposed I am. His cheeks redden and he turns around. "Thank you." I say, grabbing for my backpack and pulling out clothes. I slide a thick sweater over my head and observe my wound before pulling the hem down to my waist. "Should I clean this, or wrap it? It isn't healing anymore." I ask him.

"It'll take longer to heal because of how long it took to kill the one that scratched you. How did you take the first one down?" He asks.

"You can turn around now. I caught them off guard, they had just knocked on the door when I stabbed the one. After that I couldn't catch a break until you showed up. So, thanks, I guess."

"You're welcome." Zagreus turns to face me again. I feel like it has been years since we've seen each other.

"Why do you look older?" I ask him. "Can you change your appearance like Aph can?"

"Aph? Oh, you mean Aphrodite, don't you? I should have known she was here." He rolls his eyes.

"Yeah, so, can you?" I ask again.

"If I can, I can't control it. I age just like a human would, if not a little faster. If my father decides to kill me again, I'll start the aging process over again.

"You look two years older." I tell him.

"Okay, so a lot faster than a human might. But I think once I get to a certain age I stop. It's been a while since I've been full grown though, so I can't remember." He explains, I raise my eyebrows before looking down.

"Rose, you can't keep doing this." He says, scooting a little closer to me. "You can't keep putting yourself in danger because you feel guilty for losing Andrew."

"You don't know how I feel." I spit.

"Of course, I do! You aren't the only one who lost him. I

should have never let him come with us in the first place. It's my fault. It is all my fault."

"So, we agree then." I mutter.

"I didn't just lose him down there either, I lost *you* too. I lost the only two people in the world who *actually*liked to be around me. Don't tell me that I don't know what guilt is, or how guilty you feel, because I can see it on your face. Just like I see it on mine." I don't know why, but I pull him in for a hug and wrap my arms sternly around his torso. At first, he doesn't hug me back, but after a moment I feel his shoulders relax and his arms wrap around me tightly. Sweet smells of cinnamon and vanilla fill my nose and tears begin to slide down my face.

I missed him more than I ever wanted to admit.

I missed Zagreus so much, it was destroying me. He was right. We didn't only lose Andrew, we lost each other. We lost the only other person that could relate to the journey we had taken. I never should have cut him out of my life like I had.

"I'm sorry." He says, "I'm sorry I offered to erase your memory."

"It's okay, I know you were just trying to protect me." I tell him. I don't want to let go. I could stay wrapped in his arms for the rest of my life and be perfectly fine every second of it. But he pulls away and brushes the hair out of my face before wiping the tears from my cheeks.

"What are we going to do now?" I ask him.

"You need to go home. Your family needs to know that you're okay."

"Not going to happen." I tell him sternly.

"Rose."

"Don't try to talk me out of it, if there are more of these things then I need to get rid of them." I tell him.

"Fine." He stands to leave, not making eye contact with me. I watch him open the door and then stop, facing me again. "I got this for you." He pulls a small bag from his pocket and tosses it to me. I struggle to retrieve it from the air, it almost slips between my hands, but I catch the bag by its drawstrings. When I look back up, Zagreus is gone.

I wake up to the ceiling dripping onto my forehead. I pull the blankets around myself, suddenly freezing, before realizing that I'm drenched in sweat, not rainwater. A moment later I realize I'm not in the fort at all, but back in my bedroom at home. I jolt up out of bed. How did I get here? When did I get here? What is going on?

"She's got a cold." I hear dads voice from the hallway.

"A cold? Dad, we don't get sick." Nix tells him.

"She has a scar on her side, likely from the Vry. Her body must be so focused on healing the scratch marks that it's ignoring everything else. Her immune system is compromised because of that. She has a cold." Dad explains to him. The door opens and they both walk in, obviously surprised to see me awake. Dad has a steaming bowl of soup in his hands. "Girl, you have a lot of explaining to do." He tells me and hands over the bowl. It's tomato soup, my favorite.

I relay to them the entirety of events that took place, sneaking out, hiding out in the fort, tracking the scent of the monsters until I found them, running into Zagreus, and finally the fight. They listen quietly and patiently as I slurp down the contents of the soup bowl. They don't even ask questions.

I drain the rest of the soup and look up at them, "That's it."

"Man, I can't believe you went without me!" Nix groans, only to get an intimidating look from our father.

"How did I get back here?" I ask, Dad and Nix exchange worried looks.

"You just showed up, you were delirious. You couldn't talk or anything and you just collapsed on the doorstep." Nix says although something about his tone makes me feel like he is lying. "Dad was out driving around looking for you and made the rest of us stay here in case you came back." I don't even remember leaving the fort, I can't remember anything after Zagreus left.

"How long ago?" I ask.

"Yesterday." Dad answers me.

"Was Zagreus with me?"

"No, we haven't seen him. Rose, it's possible he was never with you in the first place."

"You think I was imagining him?"

"It's possible. You were completely out of it when you showed up, it could have been the venom from the Vry making you hallucinate him or something." Nix tries to explain.

"No, He was there."

"Rose, we haven't seen him in months, why would he just show up out of the blue for an hour and then take off again?" Nix Asks.

"I have proof." I pull the blankets off myself and check my pockets for the tiny bag Zagreus had given me, when they come up empty, I search for my bag. "Where is my bag?" I ask them.

"Downstairs, I'll go get it. Stay here." Nix tells me and runs out of the room. A moment later he's back in the room and hands me my bag. I dump the contents of the bag onto my bed and dig through them before I come up with the tiny black leather bag. I hadn't looked closely at it before, but now I notice the drawstrings are golden and there is a golden symbol stamped into the bag, it's an apple tree, with a snake around the base of it. I hand it over to my dad and he looks it over.

"What's inside?" He asks.

I shrug, "I never got around to opening it." He opens the bag and drops out the contents into my hands. It's a bracelet. The band is made of the same black leather that the bag is and two charms hang from the band. One charm is a silver wolf, the other is some kind of stone. The stone is almost perfectly round with a pearly opaque finish.

"Moonstone." Dad tells me. "Your mothers wedding ring had some moonstone in it."

"I told you I wasn't hallucinating." I glare at both my dad and Nix.

Dad brushes my glare away, "We'll discuss everything that happened when you get a little more rest. Rest that isn't forced by exhaustion." He tells me, Nix looks like he's going to argue but Dad basically pushes him out of my room and closes the door.

Left on my own, I go over to the window and look outside. It's such a surreal feeling, sleeping for so long that you don't know what day it is anymore. It makes life feel less real, like I don't even have a grasp on everything that is going on around me. The sun feels nice on my skin, but the rays are sinking behind the mountains. I hold the bracelet up in the window and admire the moonstone as it sparkles in the sunlight. Why did Zagreus give me this and where did he get it? I've never really been the jewelry type, unless you count earrings, but I forget about them most of the time anyway. I slip the leather band around my wrist, its lighter than it looks, but I'm not used to having some-thing so bulky on my arms and who knows if it'll break the next time I turn into a wolf. I slip the bracelet off and hide it under my pillow, feeling the need to keep it close to me.

I wake up in a cold sweat, once again unaware of where I am. I thrash around my bed for a moment before I realize that I'm still at home. Still safe. But the house is eerily quiet, I can't hear anything, not the tv, no voices or footsteps, almost like everyone in the house left. I creep out of bed still shivering and throw a blanket around my shoulders. I search Deme's room first, but its empty, same with Nix's room. I head for the stairs, a few of the step's creak so I make sure to avoid them as someone at the front door knocks. I freeze in my tracks. The Vry are dead right? I killed them and Zagreus would be hunting any left. Is it safe to answer the door? Another knock. Okay, it's a real person at the door. Maybe everyone was being as cautious as I was and waited for the second knock as well, but I still don't hear any movement within the house. I skulk over to the door, waiting for another knock to come, and it does. I brace myself for the worst and open the door. I instantly lose my breath.

This is a trick.

A dirty trick.

Maybe I am hallucinating. I must be, there's no other

explanation, because standing in the doorway, looking lost and frightened is my best friend, Andrew Palmer.

"Rose! Thank God, you need to help me. I don't know what's going on." He doesn't move an inch and neither do I. This must be the Vry, or something else messing with me. Andrew was taken by Persephone. He was in the Underworld, unable to come home. Even Zagreus told me that we couldn't save him.

There is no way that Andrew is actually here.

5

Hallucinations

I want to believe that Andrew is here. Every ounce of my being is screaming at me to hug him, to tell him that I'm sorry for leaving him. But my brain is telling me to stop and think. I go over everything that I know about him in my head. The scar on his chin from when he fell on the blacktop in elementary school is faintly there, his long locs make up the man-bun that sits on top of his head, but he looks different. He seems paler, and there is more fear behind his eyes than I have ever seen before. I want to believe its him, but my instincts tell me otherwise.

"Rose, please let me in. I don't know where else to go. My house was empty, I couldn't find my parents." He starts telling me, and he's right. Andrew wouldn't have anywhere to go. His parents went back to the base his dad is stationed at. They did keep the house, though. Once full of joy and love, now it sits empty and lifeless. Almost like a tomb of the friendship we once had.

"How do I know it's really you?" I ask him, I feel paralyzed in place.

"Wait, what?" His face falls, "How could you ask that? Of course, it's me. We grew up together, I drive you to school every day, we've been best friends since childhood. Did you lose your memory again?" His eyes are tearing up and I feel incredibly guilty for not believing him, but I have to make sure that I'm not being messed with. "You were a ladybug for Halloween for four years straight because you loved them so much, you wrote a short story about one in elementary school. Nix used to pretend to be a zombie and hide under your bed to scare us when he babysat for our parents." Andrew starts going on and on about all these times when we were younger, and I start bawling before I wrap my arms around him in a bear hug and pull him inside.

"I can't believe you're here, I tried to go back for you but... how did you get out, how did you come home? What did they do to you? Where were you? Gabby..." I trail off, obviously I've overloaded his brain with questions. Gabby thinks he's dead, his mom, his dad, everyone thinks he's dead.

"She thinks I'm dead, doesn't she?" He asks, following my train of thought.

"I... I didn't know what to do. Zagreus, he took control, erased everyone's memories, and made them think..." I can't finish my sentence; it seems too harsh to say out loud in front of him.

"It's all your fault." Andrew whispers and I freeze.

"I didn't...I'm—."

"It's all your fault!" Andrew turns on me and grabs me by the throat. His eyes grow darker, and he shoves me into the wall, still holding my throat. I grab at his hands but he's stronger than me and I can't get a grip on him. Tears pour from my eyes, and I try to speak but I can't. "You left me there to rot, Rose! Look! Look at what you did to me!" He yells, his skin begins to dry out and crack on his face. I close my eyes not willing to look at him anymore.

"Look at me!" Zagreus shouts. I open my eyes, instead of Andrew standing in front of me, Zagreus has his hands around my throat. "You ruined everything!" He squeezes my neck harder, and my vision begins to fade. The person in front of me begins to morph again, it becomes Nix, Deme, my dad, Aphrodite, Gabby, Jessica and finally Tyler before I run out of oxygen and my vision fades into blackness.

I wake up in a cold sweat to thunder rolling through the night sky outside of my window. Tears are pouring out of my eyes and I'm breathing heavily. A nightmare. It was only a nightmare. I'm safe at home, in my room, in my bed. But it's quiet, I can't hear anything in the house, not the tv, no voices or footsteps. It's just like the nightmare, the house feels empty, like everyone left without me. I decide to search the house, but I change the order in which I check the rooms. I check Nix's room first, and then Deme's, but both are empty again. I look at the stairs, if I go down there and there's a knock at the door I'm going straight up to my bedroom and locking the door. I take the first few steps slowly, this time making sure to step on the creaky stairs and making noise when I can. I stop on the middle of the staircase and stare at the front door. I wait for the knock, but it never comes. I wait even longer, maybe fifteen minutes but still nothing, so I begin to descend the staircase; that's when I hear the whispers.

"—wake her. We have to."

"She's sick, not in her right mind. Who knows how she'll react?"

"We can't keep this from her."

I hesitantly peek around the corner into the living room, Deme, Nix, and Aph have their backs to me. But I don't pay any attention to what they're doing, because sitting on the couch in front of them, staring straight at me is my best friend.

"Rose!" Andrew shouts and stands; I try to step back up the stairs but miss it and fall instead.

"Rose!" Deme yells and comes over to my side, "Are you okay?" She asks. I shuffle backwards into the wall.

"Stay back, you're not real. None of you are real. I'm asleep. I need to wake up." I panic. She moves closer to me, and I flinch again, she takes a step back.

"Rose, I'm real, we're all real. You're awake and you're safe." Deme tells me, but it's something she would say regardless of if I was dreaming or not. I pull my knees into my chest and hold them tightly.

"Wake up, Rose. This is a dream. He's not really here. Wake up. Wake up. Wake up." I tell myself and close my eyes. I hear heavier footsteps make their way over to me and my eyes snap open. "Stay back. Don't come near me, Nix. I mean it." I tell Nix as he approaches me.

"No, I've had enough of this." He tells me and keeps getting closer. I squirm into the corner of the room and hold my hand out, but he ignores it, smacking my hand out of his way as he kneels next to me. He stares into my eyes for a moment and studies my face, furrowing his brow. I look around the room, Deme, Aph and Andrew are now crowding in around me, it feels like the walls are closing in around me. "Rose, do me a favor?" Nix asks, I tilt my head in confusion, "try not to cry." He says and smacks me across the face so hard that I can't see for a minute.

"NIX!" Deme and Andrew yell at the same time.

"What? Now she knows she's awake," Nix turns to me, "Right?" I don't answer. I look around, this all feels so real, but so did my dream. And I'd felt pain in my dream, right? When I was being choked? Maybe not. The dream is already fading from my memory.

"It felt so real." I whisper.

"What did?" Deme asks me.

"My nightmare. I...I was all alone. There was a knock at the door. Andrew was there. Choked me, then turned into Zagreus. It felt so real." I explain.

"But it wasn't real, Rose. We're real, and your awake." She tells me delicately and grabs my hand.

"Oh God, I'm so sorry." I say, "But not to you." I turn to Nix. "What?"

"Why'd you hit me, jerk." I rub my cheek and he laughs.

"Someone had to do it, and I've already done it once." He chuckles, I stick my tongue out at him.

"So, Andrew is really here."

"Yes, It's really him." Deme squeezes my hand. I look at Andrew, really take him in. Every ounce of my being is screaming at me that this isn't real, that I'm still dreaming. I go over everything that I know about him in my head. The scar on his chin from when he fell on the blacktop in elementary school is faintly there, his long locs messily make up the man-bun that sits on top of his head, but he looks different. He seems paler, and there is more fear behind his eyes than I have ever seen before.

"Oh god, what did they do to you?" I ask him while I fight back tears.

"Let's all go back to the living room, and we can talk about it." Deme smiles and helps me up off the floor and we make our way to the couch.

"This is real, isn't it?" I ask Deme.

"Very real." She assures me. She sits me down on the couch in the middle of her and Aph, the boys take the other couch across from us.

A knock on the front door sends my body into shock. I jump back, pulling my legs up to my chest and cover my face with my hands. I can't take any more surprises. Deme puts her arms around me and Aph puts a hand on my knee.

"You're fine, don't be such a drama queen." Aph tells me. "It's only Zagreus." I pull my hands from my eyes.

"How do you know that?" I ask her.

She shrugs, "Just do." Nix gets up and goes to the door. It opens and I hear footsteps approach the living room.

"Do you have some like sixth sense for other Gods or something?" Nix asks her as he walks into the room, followed by Zagreus. There is a cut on his left eyebrow that I didn't notice before, it's still bleeding.

"I came as soon as I heard." Zagreus states, he looks back and forth from me and Andrew a few times. "What's going on? Why do you look so terrified, and why is your face red?" He asks me, wiping the blood from his brow.

"She's been hallucinating thanks to your fathers' minions, Nix hit her. Andrews real. All caught up." Aph says flatly like she's bored.

"You hit her again!" Zagreus gets in Nix's face.

"Again?" Andrew asks.

"Woah, calm down!" Deme yells getting in between the two boys. I pay no attention. Andrew is staring at the floor, muttering something to himself.

"What happened to you?" I ask him, everyone else quiets down at my voice.

"I..." He starts over, "I don't know." He sighs.

"Where did they keep you? I looked everywhere for you; nobody would tell me where you were." Zagreus tells him.

"I don't know. They force fed me those purple flowers. Everything is hazy."

"The lotus flowers don't cause memory loss, he's lying." Aph states, Zagreus glares at her.

"Dissociative Amnesia." I whisper.

"Like what you had?" Deme asks me.

"Yes, it brought on by trauma, they tortured him." I say loud enough for everyone to hear.

"I mean it makes sense, I was only locked in a secret dungeon, and I kept all my memories. Why wouldn't the kid who looks exactly like he did when he left, lose his memories?" Nix states sarcastically.

"Shut up, Nix." I roll my eyes at him.

"I do know one thing." Andrew chimes in, "I can't go outside during the day. Burns."

Aphrodite sits up, "Burns?" she looks excited and angry at the same time. "Those idiots."

"What do you mean, Aph." I ask, she's staring daggers at Zagreus now.

"You know what they did to him, you have to." She accuses him and ignores me completely.

"I don't know anything, why are you even here in the first place Aphrodite? You don't belong here."

"My business is no matter to you. Hades and Persephone have killed us all! When he finds out, we're all doomed." She spits at him.

"I have no idea what you're talking about lady. Back off."

Aphrodite sits up and the corners of her mouth curl up in a smile so sinister it's almost like I'm not even looking at the same person. "They've turned him." She sneers.

Zagreus's face goes blank, his skin pales and he looks at Andrew. "They wouldn't. No, they couldn't."

I stand up, "What the hell is going on, what did they do?" I ask them both, neither of them looks at me. Neither of them say anything.

"They didn't mean to, they tortured me, I did it. They took credit." Andrew says and everyone turns to look at him, "they said I knew too much for a human. It's a loophole."

"What are you talking about?" I demand desperately.

"I...they turned me...I'm—" Andrew stutters.

"A vampire." Aphrodite finishes for him. Her eyes twinkle against the light.

"V...Vampire." I breathe shakily, "he can't... he can't be. Not Andrew." The world shakes around me, my knees are unable to carry my weight anymore and I fall to the carpet. The world seems like it's moving in slow motion. Nobody moves at first. Zagreus grabs my arm, attempting to catch me, but it happens so suddenly not even he could see it coming. My vision blurs and I focus on the way Zagreus's hand feels around my arm.

Vampire.

Andrew is a *vampire*.

You left him there. *This is all your fault.* He's dead because of you.

What does this even mean? How did this even happen? How can there be zombie-vampires and regular vampires? Everyone in the room is moving now. Zagreus lifts me up and pulls me into him, I don't fight it. I let all my weight lean into him, a cloud of cinnamon and vanilla cologne swirling around my head. Aphrodite is smiling bigger than I've ever seen, Deme is looking at me, Nix is staring at Andrew, and Andrew is staring at the floor. I still don't know where dad is, he should be here shouldn't he? Maybe I'm still dreaming, maybe this isn't real either. Just my brain messing me up, my body fighting the infection and the cold. Zagreus rubs the back of my head lightly; he's supporting most of my weight still. I shuffle next to him, attempting to carry my own weight but he grabs my arm and stops me.

"Don't. You'll fall." He grabs me tighter.

"No, I'll be okay now. Promise." I tell him and pull away again, but as I do, the world seems to shift around us. The living room falls into the ground and lava fills the room. The walls crack away and splash into the boiling hot liquid. I'm standing on a cliff now, with Zagreus still holding onto my arm. I look up at him, only to find that Zagreus is gone, and Tyler is now holding my arm.

"You'll pay for what you did." He says, although for some reason it's not his voice that I hear. I can't place the voice either. He stares at me for a long moment before a wicked smile spreads across his face and he shoves me with all his weight. I fall for what feels like forever, staring up at Tyler who is now laughing maniacally, until I get swallowed by darkness.

6

No Care

I sit up. I'm in a hospital room, the thin paper sheets over me do nothing to keep me warm and a heart monitor beeps quietly next to me. Across from me is a window that looks into the hallway, outside of it are two people, although I can't make out their faces through the blinds one of them is a red head, the other has pastel blue hair. I know who they are I just can't place their names inside of my head and before I can get a closer look at them, both people are gone; almost like they weren't there at all. Underneath the window sitting in an armchair that looks like it was ripped out of the nineties, is Zagreus. He's sleeping, I think, I mean his eyes are closed but I don't know if he's pretending or not. He hasn't moved since I've woken up and his back was towards the window so he wouldn't have been able to see who those two people were. How did I even get here? And why is Zagreus here? I don't even know if anything that happened last night was real.

"Are you awake?" I ask him, his eyes pop open and he sits up.

"Oh my god, you're up! I—" He starts but the door next to him bursts open and in walks the last person I expected to see.

"Rose! I was so worried about you. Are you okay? What happened?" Gabby looks like she hasn't slept in days. There are dark circles under her eyes and her jet-black hair is messily hanging around her neck. I look at Zagreus and back at her before I realize that she is also staring at Zagreus. "Wait, why are *you* here? Didn't you move or something?" She asks him bluntly.

"Gabby, how did you know I was here?" I ask her, ignoring her puzzled expression.

"My mom is a nurse here, remember? And you didn't answer my question." She tells me before turning back to Zagreus, expecting an answer.

"I was in town, visiting and I heard what happened." Zagreus explains to her quickly. She doesn't look like she believes him, but she turns back to me.

"I thought you were—well you don't really wanna know what I thought, I'm just glad you're okay." She tells me. Gabby must've thought that I'd gotten sick with the "disease" that was spreading around town, she probably thought I was dying.

"I don't actually know how I got here, what happened?" I look at Zagreus to answer me. If I'm at the hospital, there must be some reason why.

"You were sick, had a hundred-degree fever for a few days. Your dad is down at the cafeteria with your brother and sister. I got here this morning, went to your house as you guys were heading here, you were pretty out of it, so I'm not surprised you don't remember." He tells me. I still don't know what is going on though, one minute I'm in the living room being told that Andrew is a vampire and the next I'm falling into lava and waking up in the hospital, but I can't ask about anything with Gabby standing right here. I need to get her to leave somehow.

"Rosey! You're awake, that's—Oh shit," Andrew walks up behind Gabby in the doorway, the last time he saw her she was blonde, so he didn't recognize her, but she knew his voice immediately. Gabby spins so fast and comes face to face with him.

"No. You can't. You're not." She stammers, "You're supposed to be dead." She finally gets out. She turns again and looks at me, her expression makes me feel like I've been stabbed in the gut, like I've betrayed her. Before I even have a second to try to explain what is going on or even process it myself, Gabby turns to Andrew again and slaps him straight across the face.

"Yeah, I deserved that." Andrew states shutting the door behind him and locking it, "Look guys I can't lie to her. We have to tell her the truth." He speaks. Zagreus doesn't say anything. I've been wanting to tell her the truth since the beginning, but it isn't my secret to tell. Zagreus turns to Gabby. In one swift motion he claps his hands together and presses his index finger to her forehead.

"You will not remember anything for the next two minutes." He tells her and all expression leaves her face, her body goes limp, and she seems dead.

"What did you just do?" Andrew asks him. I start counting down the seconds.

One-fifty-nine, one-fifty-eight, one-fifty-seven.

Zagreus paces the room, "What did *I* just do? What did *you* do? What were you thinking, we can't tell her anything?"

"Why not?" Andrew asks.

"Oh I don't know, maybe the end of the world as we know it?"

"Ares doesn't have to know." Andrew tells him which sends Zagreus into a spiral.

"What? You think your new gal-pal Aphrodite isn't going to go crawling back to him with everything she knows the second she gets a chance to? Or that Hades and Persephone won't come up with some other *loophole* and turn your girlfriend into a Gorgon or something? There is absolutely no way that we get around this." He's pacing faster now, and Andrew won't even look at him as he tries to think of a response.

One-thirty, one-twenty-nine, one-twenty-eight, one-twenty-seven, one-twenty-six.

"Well, maybe Aphrodite doesn't need to know, what if we don't tell anyone outside of this room?" Andrew asks him, Zagreus stops walking.

"We don't even know how she is going to react to hearing the truth, Andrew. We can't risk telling her, she's just a human, find a way to live without her."

"She's his soulmate, Zagreus. Easier said than done." I tell him.

"She's my—what?" Andrew looks shocked and I realize that aside from Aphrodite, I'm the only one who knows this.

"That's what Aph told me." I shrug. Zagreus sends a glare at me.

"It doesn't matter, she can't know, and you can't tell her."

"Then what are we going to do with her then? Erase her memory so she forgets that she saw me and then what? I can't go outside, its still daylight, and you can't just put her out in the hallway like a lost puppy, her mom works here and told her that Rose is a patient, she'll come back here, and we'll have to deal with this all over again." Andrew begins to tap his foot impatiently; I can't even remember the last time I saw him this annoyed.

"We can hide you in the bathroom." Zagreus suggests.

Andrew narrows his eyes, "What if she needs to go to the bathroom? Or someone else does? Where am I going to hide then?" He asks.

Thirty-four, thirty-three, thirty-two, thirty-one.

Zagreus groans, "I don't know, okay. But your argument for her knowing the truth about us can't be that you don't want to hide in the bathroom.

"Yes, it can." Andrew crosses his arms and stands completely still, waiting for Zagreus to challenge him. They stare daggers at each other for a few seconds, neither of them budging, but they only have a few seconds left until—,

"The truth about what?" Gabby asks, the two boys freeze in place, not ready for their two minutes to be up already, but I don't waste a second.

I take a deep breath "That I'm a werewolf, Areon is really the Greek God, Zagreus who is the son of Hades and Persephone, and Andrew didn't really go missing or die six months ago. He was *actually* being held hostage by Persephone that whole time because they were originally holding a bunch of other werewolves' captive, including my brother Nix, but we set them free, so while we were escaping, she locked down the underworld somehow and Zagreus forced me to leave without Andrew and then Nix knocked me out because I refused to come home with them. Does that cover everything? Oh, Aph is really the Greek Goddess Aphrodite, and she was dating Ares, but they broke up, so for some crazy reason, she decided to see what high school was like and moved in with me. Deme's powers as an oracle just awakened, and the dead people aren't dead because they were sick, well they are in a way I guess, but they're being killed by these things called the Vrykolokas that I hunted down and that's why I'm sick because I got scratched by one and my body isn't healing right, but Andrew showed up on my doorstep yesterday and now he's a vampire apparently. It's also like super against the Gods rules for you to know about any of this, by the way and that's what these two were fighting about, and that's basically all that I know." Not a single person in the room moves as I blurt out everything, but I couldn't stop when I started telling her about everything. It all just pours out of my mouth like the water at Niagara Falls. Gabby doesn't say anything, but the look on her face does, she doesn't know if she believes me or not and honestly, I wouldn't believe me if I was her. Andrew looks ecstatic but also like he's trying to hide the fact that he is and Zagreus looks both angry and scared at the same time, like Ares is just going to appear out of thin air and cut off our heads in one swift swing of his arms.

Andrew pulls on the cord of the blinds but only one side goes up while the other goes down, he fumbles with the cord for a second and a doctor passes by the window and gives him a funny look. Finally, he pulls both strings and fixes his mistake before turning the wand to close the blinds fully.

"Rose." Is all Zagreus can manage to say, he opens and shuts his mouth in disbelief for more than a few minutes. "How... How could you do that?"

"Easy. None of this is real anyway." I tell him.

"Wha—wait, what do you mean none of this is real?" He asks me.

"I mean that I'm hallucinating again and I'm going to wake back up and still be in the fort in a minute or something and I'm sick of lying to her, it doesn't matter if she isn't real, at least I told her the truth."

"Rose, this is real. You are really here in the hospital."

"Prove it."

"How am I supposed to prove to you that I'm real and not just a figment of your imagination?"

"I don't know." I shrug, Andrew and Gabby still haven't said a word. Gabby still looks like she's in shock and Andrew for once just looks like he doesn't know what to say. Zagreus paces for a few moments, he stops to look at me, shakes his head and continues pacing. I get comfortable in my hospital bed, messing with the buttons that lift my head up and down. Zagreus approaches me and I look up at him. He looks scared for some reason, although I have absolutely no idea why until he's leaning down, his face a mere inches away from mine. His breath is warm on my cheeks, his nose is so close to mine that we're basically touching. Zagreus leans in to kiss me so suddenly, I don't realize it's happening until it's too late. It feels like every ounce of my body is alive, tingling with excitement. I don't want to, but I pull away from him and slap him firmly on the cheek, but he doesn't even flinch or move away. My heartbeat on the monitor is beeping quickly and I can feel my cheeks turning red.

"Do you still think you're hallucinating?" He whispers, still close enough to touch. I don't respond to him though, instead I look away from him at Gabby. She's smiling now and I roll my eyes at her and turn to Andrew, who is also grinning from ear to ear. Zagreus finally backs away and leans up against the wall, he crosses his arms and looks at Gabby. "So, what are we going to do about you?" He asks the room.

"I won't tell anyone." Gabby mutters, she's fiddling with her hands. "I mean, this is all a lot to take in, but if you're telling the truth—and even if you aren't telling the truth, I won't say anything to anyone."

"It doesn't matter if you don't tell anyone—,"

"Just give her a chance. If Ares finds out, or Aphrodite tells him, it doesn't matter anyway. He isn't going to come looking for proof, he doesn't seem like the type to investigate. He'll end the world and ask questions later." I cut Zagreus off. He avoids eye contact with me, but he nods. "Hades and Persephone already risked it when they sent the Vry here." I add.

"They didn't send them." Zagreus tells me, "They wouldn't have sent me to hunt them if they did. This wasn't meant to happen."

"Well, I need some answers then. I need the truth."

"What do you mean?" He asks.

"Hades didn't send the Vry? Andrews a vampire? I don't even know how I got here, when did I pass out? What parts were real and what parts weren't?" I explain.

"You thought you were dreaming when you came downstairs, you weren't. Everything up until you fell was real, I told you what they turned me into, and you just collapsed, Zagreus had to catch you, but you were out cold after that." Andrew explains, "You started convulsing and we brought you to the hospital, your dad met us here later. You needed a guardian to approve treatment, so he had to cut his trip short."

"His trip?" I ask.

"He'll explain later. It's not my place to tell you." Andrew says, Gabby starts to get up from her chair and head towards the door, but Zagreus cuts her off.

"Where do you think you're going?" He spits.

"I...I just wanted to get some fresh air." She explains, her body language is all over the place. She is still shuffling her hands and her posture is terrible.

"I'm sorry, but you can't go anywhere alone now."

"What, why?" She meets his eyes for a moment before looking back down at the floor.

"It's not safe from now on, you need to stay with us."

"I'll come back. I promise."

"It's not that I don't trust you, I don't trust anyone else." Zagreus explains to her, "We don't know where the Vry came from, we don't know who sent them. At this point, anyone could be an enemy. None of us can be alone." He makes eye contact with me, "*none of us.*" He repeats.

"So, all of us are stuck here until nightfall then?" I ask Andrew.

"No, he can go out into the sunlight, he just can't be out there for too long or it'll drain him, we need to get him some sustenance too, or he'll be too dangerous for you to be around." Zagreus answers for him.

"*Sustenance?*"

"Seemed like a better word choice than fresh-squeezed blood." Zagreus winks at me.

I hold back the urge to gag, "Thanks for that."

"I can get it." Gabby pipes up, she's suddenly full of energy.

"Get what?" Andrew asks her.

"The blood." She states, "It'll prove I'm on your side, that I can handle knowing the truth. I can ask my mom where they store the donations and get some for you."

"While I appreciate the offer, I plan on keeping him on a strict animal only diet." Zagreus says, "We keep cow blood in the Underworld for this reason, I can just pop down there and get it. I'm assuming that's what my parents fed you?" He asks Andrew.

"Why do you have cows' blood in the Underworld?" I ask

"Persephone can't leave for most of the year and Hades doesn't like to, we have to have some kind of agriculture or there's no food." I notice he doesn't say what the blood is for though.

Andrew shrugs, "I didn't really ask what I was being fed, but I don't remember anyway."

There's a light knock on the door, Andrew peaks out the window and unlocks the door. Deme, Nix, and my father all file into the room.

"Glad to see you're up, we were just about to head out. I've got some business to work out." My dad says.

"Doing what?" I ask him. He sighs.

"There's been some new developments with the werewolves you freed, some of them had nowhere to go and ultimately ended up homeless. I've been working on employing some of the older ones, in return for their work I'm letting them stay in some of the empty housing developments I've been working on. But it isn't so easy for the younger ones, they need school and a stable living situation, but can't be placed in the care of regular foster homes because of their training. They've all been wolves for so long that they haven't adjusted well."

"How awful." I say.

"Yeah, I've been attempting to locate their families to no prevail, but I need to get back to them soon. So, we need to have a serious talk for a minute." My dad tells us, he gives Gabby a funny look but doesn't question her presence. "Welcome back to the land of the living, boy." He pats Andrew on the back, "Although I'm told you require a strict raw diet now."

"We have Andrew's food source covered for now," Zagreus tells my dad.

"Good, that's one less thing to worry about." Dad comes over to my bedside. "Doctors say you are good to go, they've prescribed some antibiotics to fight infection, and some over-the-counter cold meds for your cold. Told them your scratches were from when you fainted, so if they ask, don't push it more than that."

I pull the blankets up to cover my bottom half and

pull the hospital gown up to reveal my side, "They're almost healed anyway, shouldn't be a problem." I tell him.

He nods, "We still have a few of these creatures out there, the morgue was missing a few bodies, so you need to be on guard still." He tells us.

"They won't stop coming until we figure out who sent them in the first place," Zagreus explains, "Hades wouldn't send the Vrykolakas to build an army, they can be unreliable and move too slow to build the kind of army he wants."

"Then why kidnap a handful of werewolves if he wants more numbers?" Nix asks.

"It wasn't about starting a war with the wolves; it was about taking something of Zeus's and making them into his own." Zagreus tells him, Nix rolls his eyes and mumbles something, but I don't catch it.

"Well now that we know someone is controlling the Vry, our best bet to stopping this is to find them and take them out. No more hunting the Vry until then. We don't want the numbers going up, but we don't want to be put out of commission like this again." Dad says, he pulls his flip phone out of his pocket and checks the time, "I need to head out, are you guys okay on your own?" He asks.

"I'll keep an eye on them." Zagreus states. I can't help but roll my eyes at him.

"Get dressed and you can leave, I've already signed your release papers." Dad says before leaving the room.

I go into the bathroom to change while Andrew and Gabby go searching for a jacket in the lost in found that he can wear to cover his skin when we leave. I look like garbage; my hair is knotting, and I have dark purple half-moons under my eyes. I strip out of the hospital gown and examine the scratches on my side again, they haven't changed, but the bruising around them is slowly disappearing along with some of the other bruises on my arms and legs. I pull on the clothes that Deme brought for me to change into since the nurses decided to shred my shirt and shorts, I was wearing so they could get me into the gown. I ball up the hospital dress and throw it into the designated bag in the corner of the bathroom and head out the door.

A nurse is standing outside of the bathroom with a wheelchair.

"All set?" He asks.

"That's not for me, is it?" I ask him.

"You're a fall risk. Hospital policy." He tells me with a smile. I groan and get into the chair; the nurse releases the break on the chair and begins to wheel me towards the door.

"We'll be right behind you; Deme is pulling Gabby's car up." Zagreus tells me.

I get wheeled through the hospital, down to ground level and through the big sliding glass doors out front. It's sunset, without a window in my room I had no idea what time of day it was. Deme has the car idling and she's waiting by the passenger side with the door open.

"Where's Gabby?" I ask her as the nurse sets the breaks on the wheelchair and helps me out.

"They'll be out in a sec." She tells me while taking hold of my arm from the nurse and helping me into the front seat. "Thank you for your help!" She says sweetly to the nurse, and he nods.

"Can't park out here too long, make sure your friends are quick." He tells us as he turns the chair around and begins to wheel it back into the hospital. Zagreus and Nix come out of the doors as the nurse walks in, and Gabby and Andrew follow behind them a few seconds later. Deme shuts the car door and gets into the backseat with Nix while Zagreus opens the hatch in the back. Andrew makes a run for it and jumps into the trunk of the car.

"Little dramatic, but okay." Zagreus says as he drapes a blanket over him and shuts the hatch. Gabby gets into the driver's seat; Zagreus loads up in the back with Nix and Deme.

"Everyone ready?" Gabby asks, she's starting to sound like her old self again.

We pull into my driveway fifteen minutes later. Gabby backs in perfectly, with the back of the car facing the front door and shuts the car off. We all sit in silence for a second together, listening to the crickets as they begin to chirp.

"I don't know about you guys, but I'm going to get heat stroke if I sit under this blanket any longer." Andrew calls out from the back his voice muffled from all of the layers on top of him. Gabby and I look at each other and start laughing. It feels good to lose control for a second, and our laughter becomes infectious, soon everyone in the car is laughing too.

"What? What's so funny?" Andrew desperately calls out to us, but it only makes us laugh harder.

Our laughter soon resides, and we begin to unload the car and head inside. Everyone settles into the living room and Nix flips on the television, leaving it on some true crime show. We all watch it in silence, getting through half of the episode before Andrew starts shuffling in his seat.

"Am I always going to be like this?" He asks no one in particular, he's staring at the wall.

"What do you mean?" I ask him.

"Like, is there a cure?" He asks and we all look at Zagreus.

"Not that I know of, becoming a Vampire isn't exactly easy." He speaks.

"But how does it work exactly? Where did they come from?" I ask.

"It's kind of a long story."

"I think we have time." Deme says.

"Okay, well the very first vampire wasn't born one, he was an Italian man named Ambrogio. Ambrogio was an adventurer, and he traveled to Greece sometime in early four-hundred BC. It was his dream to have his fortune told by the legendary Oracle of Delphi at the temple of Apollo and upon seeing him, the Oracle only muttered a cryptic phrase to him: 'The curse. The moon. The blood will run.' And—,"

"Wait, that sounds familiar. Didn't—," I start.

"I said that. On Halloween. It was the first time I didn't speak gibberish after having a vision." Deme says.

"It must've been the night Andrew was turned. Your Ancestor was the one who originally gave that prophecy, for you to state it again isn't a coincidence." Zagreus explains. "Anyway,

Ambrogio was so disturbed by the message that he spent the night outside of the temple. When morning came, a beautiful maiden appeared, the sister of the Oracle, Selene, who came to the temple every morning to care for her sister who couldn't leave and the temple she was forced to live in.

Ambrogio fell in love with Selene and would meet her every morning, until the day he asked for her hand in marriage and asked her to return to Italy with him. She agreed and the two were set to depart the following morning. But Apollo had also fallen in love with Selene and was enraged that a mere mortal had won her over, he cursed Ambrogio so that the touch of the sun would burn his flesh. Ambrogio ended up hiding in a cave that led to Hades, who offered him and Selene asylum in the Underworld if he could retrieve the silver bow of Artemis and return it to him. Ambrogio then hunted and killed swans for forty-five days, offering the swans to Artemis and using their blood to write poems to Selene."

"Uh-oh," Andrew mumbles.

"What's wrong?" I ask, sitting up in my chair.

"Oh, uhm... nothing. Sorry."

Zagreus narrows his eyes at him but continues, "On the forty-fifth day Ambrogio took a shot at a swan and the bow broke, feeling pity he fell to his hands and knees and wept. Artemis felt sorry for him and appeared before him where he asked to borrow her bow and arrows to shoot one final swan in her honor, she agreed. Ambrogio got his hands on the bow, but as he was running back to Hades, Artemis cursed him so that the touch of silver to his skin would burn him and cause great pain. He dropped the bow and now that he had been cursed by two

Gods, fell to his knees, and begged for mercy from Artemis. She felt pity for the man and gave him one last chance, she bestowed upon him the speed and strength of the Gods and made him as powerful a hunter as she was, she then gave him fangs so he could draw the blood of his prey to continue writing his poetry, among other things like immortality, but he would have to abandon all the other Gods except for her. Which she is chaste, so he would have to abandon his love for Selene. They could be together, but they would have to remain unmarried and could not touch each other. He agreed, and Selene and him ended up living in a cave system in the darkness so the sun wouldn't burn him, and Selene could still visit her family. But as Selene aged, Ambrogio did not. On her deathbed, Ambrogio begged Artemis to make Selene immortal as well. Artemis told him that he could touch Selene just once, to drain the blood from her body. Doing this, he would kill her mortal body, but ensure that they would stay together forever. When Ambrogio drained her blood and set her lifeless body down, he watched as her body began to radiate with light and her spirit began to rise to the heavens. Her spirit met with Artemis at the moon, which lit up at the arrival of Selene's spirit. Selene became the Goddess of moonlight and every night her rays of light would touch Ambrogio, and their children, the newly created vampires who Ambrogio could make now that his blood and Selene's were mixed."

"How tragic." Gabby sighs.

"But Ambrogio has been gone for hundreds of years, not a soul has seen him, and no new vampires have surfaced until now." Zagreus says, "It's strange."

"But didn't Aph say that Hades and Persephone turned him." I ask.

Zagreus rolls his eyes, "Aphrodite doesn't know anything. She's been brainwashed by Ares."

"I wasn't brainwashed." Aphrodite states, we all turn around and find her standing in the archway of the living room, both hands on her hips and glaring at Zagreus.

Aphrodite crosses the threshold and steps down into the living room to join us. She's no longer pretending to be a teenager; her looks have reverted to the way she was when I'd first seen her; legs for days and a killer glare. She sits on an empty armchair, crosses her legs, and holds her hands together in her lap before staring Zagreus down.

"I wasn't brainwashed, I was in love." She tells him.

"Oh really?" He asks, rolling his eyes.

"Sounds like Stockholm's" Nix snickers under his breath, but Aphrodite hears him and throws him one of her signature glares; he backs down almost immediately. *Wimp.*

"But I've grown since then." She states.

"Yeah, like two feet," Andrew jokes, Aphrodite ignores him.

"You really expect me to believe that?" Zagreus asks her.

"Why not?" She asks.

"Maybe because you're a manipulative, spoiled brat, who doesn't care about anyone other than herself." Zagreus states, Nix chokes back a laugh.

"Fine, I don't need to prove myself to you." She sneers and turns to me. "I've thought a lot about what we talked about, and I am ready to join your cause."

"My cause?" I ask.

"Yes, I will help put an end to Ares' reign." She tells me, she doesn't break eye contact with me for a second and I can't help but believe her.

"So, what does this mean, what do we do next?" I ask.

"Well, first things first, assuming you've told Gabby here, I will not be reporting that back to him. But we need to find out who is controlling these monsters and put an end to them before he finds out, or there will be no stopping him."

"How can we trust you?" Zagreus asks her.

"You can't, but considering I've been a better friend to Rose these past few months than you have, I'd say she can trust me more than she can trust you."

"What are you—," Zagreus starts.

"No, she has a point." I interrupt, he turns to me, hurt in his eyes.

"I mean, I can just leave then, if you don't need my help." He starts to get up.

"I'm not saying that." I glare at him, "You weren't here, I didn't necessarily want you here, but you didn't even try."

"I figured you wanted space." He says quietly, and I instantly become aware of the many eyes staring at the two of us. "Whatever, it doesn't matter. I'm over it, and Aph is right, we need to figure out what we are going to do about the Vry."

"Let's just go hunt them." Nix offers.

"Like that went so well last time." Zagreus says, they all look at me.

"I was doing just fine on my own." I argue.

98 ~ R.L. NELSON

"Yeah, until you got side-swiped by one and almost died."

"This isn't helping." I glare at him.

"So, say we find who is controlling the Vry, what happens then?" Deme asks.

"We kill them." Nix says.

"Uhm, no." I say.

"Well, they must pay for it. Hades isn't going to be happy they took control from him," Zagreus says. "I'll have to take whoever it is back to him with me."

"And what is he going to do to them?" I ask him.

"No idea. Depends on who it is I guess." He shrugs.

Gabby lets Nix take her car to go get food for everyone from town and he takes Deme with him. I'm not convinced she really believes everything that she's been told, but she is going along with it well considering how crazy all of this must be to her. I pull her aside once everyone leaves and we head upstairs to my bedroom for some privacy.

"I know all of this sounds pretty insane, how are you holding up?" I ask her, she sits at the vanity in my room, staring at her reflection.

"I think I'm okay," She says, "Honestly, I knew something was kind of off about you all."

"Really, how?"

"Well, I mean, Andrew went missing, your brother showed up after being missing for years and then Aph was at Andrews funeral and then living with you suddenly. It all seemed a little suspicious." She explains, "I mean, I went with it, obviously. But I think, deep down, I knew something was up."

"You saw her at the funeral?"

"Yeah, she was hard to miss."

I giggle, "She is, isn't she?"

"Yeah," she laughs with me, "But, I grew up with my grandfather telling me all these old stories about China. He immigrated here before I was born, with my mother and his wife. Although I never got to meet my grandmother, she passed away just after I was born. But he didn't want me to grow up not knowing about our ancestors; family and our Chinese heritage was so important to him. He used to tell me these stories at bedtime, there were the classics, about princesses of course, but as I got older, he would tell me darker stories. Stories about the Jiangshi, and The Wolf of Zhongshan. My mom didn't want him to, she always thought it would scare me, but it didn't. I was so interested about my country that I always begged him to tell me more. Of course, he always made everything seem more magical and happier than some of them really were, but I used to sit in the window of my bedroom, staring up at the moon, wishing I could have lived to see them all." She turns to face me, "Part of me thinks that my grandfather was preparing me for this."

"That's really sweet." I tell her.

"Yeah, it's like I get to keep a piece of my grandfather with me now, I can't walk away from that because it seems scary." A single tear falls from her eye.

A light knock on the door startles both of us, Andrew walks in silently and his eyes go wide when he realizes Gabby has been crying.

"Oh!" He rushes to her side, moving quicker than normal "is everything okay?"

Gabby wipes her cheek, "Yeah, we're good." She smiles.

"What's up?" I ask him.

"Oh, I was just hoping I could have a moment with Gabby, if that's okay."

"Yeah, we're all good." Gabby smiles at him, "We'll catch up later." She tells me and follows him out of the room.

I head back down to the living room, Zagreus is sitting on the couch, staring at the ground. Aph apparently didn't want to stick around with him, I can hear her in the basement.

"Hey." I say, sitting on the couch next to him.

"Hey." He replies, not looking up.

"You okay?" I ask.

"Fine." He says flatly, "Just thinking."

"About what?" I ask, his eyes meet mine.

"This mess we're in." He turns away from me again. I start fiddling with my hands, not sure what to say. Do I tell him that I missed him? Do I tell him I was wrong, that he shouldn't have left me alone, that I *needed* him? The words hang in the back of my throat, and I can feel my stomach turning, although that could just be from not eating anything today. Gabby had asked me months ago if I loved him, but I'm still not sure; it's not that simple.

"I missed you." He says, his eyes meeting mine again.

"I missed you too." I tell him, a small smile spreading across my face.

"I'm sorry, for everything."

I reach for his hand and hold it in mine, "Don't worry about it." I tell him. He leans back in his seat but doesn't pull his hand away.

"I wasn't ready for this." He sighs.

"Ready for what?" I ask.

"For the surface world, my dad was right."

"What do you mean?"

"He told me it would be like this. How people are complicated, it's not like the Underworld where you see someone for their soul. Here, people don't show what they feel. Emotions are complicated." He groans and shuts his eyes.

"I'm sorry."

"Don't be." He mumbles.

"No." I start again, "I'm *sorry*."

"For what?' He sits up and looks at me.

"For pushing you away. I was wrong. I was scared, and I had just lost my best friend. I didn't know what to do, so I pushed you, and everyone else away. That wasn't fair of me to do." I explain. "I know that it isn't a good excuse, but I am sorry."

"Don't worry about it." He smiles, "I'll live." He leans forward, kisses my forehead, and pulls me into a hug. I melt into him, wrapping my arms around his waist and burying my face into his neck. His warmth surrounds me, and I never want to leave his arms again.

The front door blows open sending a shock through my body. Zagreus stands in between me and the door, shielding me from whatever is about to come through.

"Nix is gone!" Deme yells as she runs into the house.

"What do you mean?" I stand and move Zagreus to my side so I can see my sister better.

"He's gone, he took off, I can't find him." She babbles, not really making sense.

"Okay, Deme, breathe." I tell her. "Slowly tell us what happened." She comes and sits on the recliner and takes a few deep breaths as Andrew comes into the room, pulling Gabby by her hand behind him.

"What's going on?" Andrew asks, "We heard a loud noise and yelling."

"Well, we went to go get pizza, you know, so we...we paid and were waiting, when he just stood up. I asked him what was wrong, but he wouldn't talk to me, he just walked out the door, so I followed him out and he just shoved me down to the ground and took off. He was gone before I could even stand up." Deme explains.

7

Man, or Monster

Deme is so upset that she is shaking. I grab a blanket and drape it around her shoulders.

"He didn't say anything to you?" I ask Deme, she's about to start crying, her eyes are welling up with tears.

"No, and I can't see anything either. I keep trying, but nothing I do is working.

"You can't force yourself to see visions, that isn't how it works." Zagreus tells her.

"Then what *use* is this stupid power then!" She yells and stands up, throwing the blanket down onto the ground, "What good am I if I can't help anyone?" She starts pacing. Everyone silently stares at her.

"Deme, it's going to be okay, we'll find him. You just got your gift; we don't expect you to be able to use it whenever we need it." I tell her, trying to calm her down.

"You and Nix have control over yours! Why is this so hard?" the tears are coming now, they stream down her cheeks like a river.

"Don't worry about it, Deme, it's okay. Everyone works at their own pace. But we need to focus on finding Nix." I tell her, "Which direction did he take off in?" I ask.

"I don't know! Its dark out and he shoved me down!" She yells.

"Where were you facing when you went outside, I just need a general direction." I explain.

"I don't know, West? towards the school maybe." She finally sits back down and takes a deep breath. "But there's like twelve different neighborhoods over there, it'll be impossible to find him." She whines.

"No, no. That helps." I tell her, and turn to everyone else, "Nix wouldn't just take off unless he heard something, and if he heard it, but Deme didn't, that means it had to be coming from farther than the next street over."

"You don't know that for sure." Andrew says.

"Yes, I do. Nix has better hearing than I do, and if it was just someone screaming from the next street over, Deme would have heard that."

"Rose, there's no way." Zagreus tells me.

"Just... trust me, okay."

"We don't even know if he heard anything, we don't know what's out there. We should plan and then go look for him." Zagreus says Andrew nods in agreement.

"He could be in trouble!" I tell them.

"He can handle himself for a little bit, he'll be fine." Zagreus assures me.

"What if it's the Vry? What if there are so many of them that he gets scratched, and they get away. You were there for me, so we should be there for him."

"That's a lot of what ifs, Rose. You *just* got out of the hospital; I can't risk you getting hurt again. Nix lied about how you got home, he followed you and fought one of the Vry when you were down. He is more than capable of taking care of himself."

"He followed me?" I ask. The branch breaking outside of the fort must have been him.

"Yes, and he was perfectly fine. You don't need to worry about him." He tells me.

"Fine." I cross my arms, and everyone relaxes a little bit.

"Thank you, let's just sit down and discuss this for a second." Zagreus says, everyone starts towards the couches, and I seize my opportunity by running out of the front door.

"I'm sorry!" I call out as I cross the porch. I ignore the stairs and leap down onto the dirt and take off running. I can hear them stumbling across the porch after me, but I transform into a wolf and cross the street as fast as I can before I cut into the neighbor's yard and jump their fence.

If Nix went towards the school, the best place for me to find him would probably be there. The school is almost fifteen miles away from my house, I should be able to make it there before Zagreus can catch up with me since I can take as many shortcuts as I want to. The best shortcut would have been to cut behind the grocery store, but the parking lot is so large I know that I can't risk it. Too many hunters live in the area, and all of them would be proud to 'take down' a wolf, so they could mount it on their walls. Instead, I try to stick to the edges of the forest. Paradise is majorly undeveloped, most of the town is covered in forest property and dead-end streets, leaving plenty of hiding spots for the homeless community and wild animals to take solace in.

I canvas the school quickly. It's eerily dark and quiet out, but I keep making my rounds around the campus. The cold winter breeze blows through the school grounds, sending a shiver down my spine. The flagpole shakes as the flag bellows in the wind. The parking lots are empty, no sign of Gabby's car anywhere; I'm not sure if that's a good sign or not. The entire campus covers a lot of ground. The middle school and high school are located directly next to each other, with only the football field and the basketball dome to separate them. All in all, I'm walking around forty acres of land, and it's taking me way too long to make my way around both campus's, add in that the high school sits on higher ground than the middle school does and the fifteen miles it took to get here and I'm giving myself quite the workout. I sit down in some brush just off the side of the road to take a break when I hear something. A deep rumbling from underground, almost like the earth is breaking open. I follow the sound, if this is what Nix heard then maybe he's at the source of it already.

I end up on the football field when the rumbling stops, but there isn't anyone around. I cross over the track and make my way to the center of the field, there is nothing there either. Most of the snow left on the grass remains untouched. I lay down in the snow and muss it up, sinking my fur into ground to cool myself off. I'm panting from exhaustion, I probably shouldn't have taken off so soon after getting out of the hospital, I feel like I haven't moved in a month and my joints feel stiff.

One by one the stadium lights turn on, each one of them pointing straight at me like a spotlight on a stage. I stand up and look around, but with the sudden harsh lighting, it's hard to make anything out. Someone is crying, I can hear their sobs on the other end of the field; but it's hard to tell who it is. Their cries get louder, and I decide to move, the spotlight moves from me to whoever is on the other end of the field.

"Rose!" Deme screams out and I pick up the pace as I run over to her, transforming back into a human as I reach her. She isn't looking at me, but at the grass below us and she's now wearing a white t-shirt covered in blood. "Why did you leave us?" She asks, "It was a trap, they wanted you to leave!" She tells me and I try to calm her by rubbing her back. But something feels wrong, like her spine is broken. Her head snaps up and she makes direct eye contact with me, but her eyes are pitch black and she has blood trails on her cheeks. "You shouldn't have left us." She speaks, her voice lower than normal. I flinch backward, not understanding what is going on, but she jumps after me and grabs me by the throat, lifting me into the air until my feet are dangling above the ground. "You shouldn't have taken him away from us." She hisses, I grab at her hands, trying to pry her fingers open from around my neck. This isn't Deme, but I don't recognize the voice, whoever this is, is strong. She laughs and throws me backwards. I hit the ground and roll, gasping for breath, but

I don't even get a second to recoup. Something big is standing behind me. I can feel its presence at my spine, as its warm breath hits the back of my neck.

I slowly turn around to face whatever is behind me. Standing tall, in his half wolf form is Nix. He swipes his hand and slams me to the ground, so hard that he knocks the wind out of me. Unable to control my breathing, I can't turn into a wolf, so I try to roll away out of his reach but he's moving at an unnatural speed and is on top of me within seconds. He grabs my throat and lifts me up before slamming me back to the ground and back up again. My legs dangle freely above the ground again, I use my hands to try and free myself from his grasp, but I can't. Instead, I kick my legs out at him, connecting my foot with his stomach before he drops me and cries out in pain—wait, no that didn't... could it have... am I seeing things?

For a split second, I swear he *flickered*, or maybe distorted. Whatever it was, for only a moment, Nix wasn't Nix. As he clutches his stomach, I take this opportunity to put some space between us so I can finally catch my breath.

I hurt him, that's what caused the flicker. Maybe if I hurt him again, I can see who it really is.

I stand as tall as I can, my throat feels like it is throbbing and I'm still breathing hard. I fought Nix once before, in the Underworld. At that point he'd been a half wolf for a while and didn't recognize who I was. I didn't want to hurt him then; it had been all about surviving and making him come to his senses. Now, I must hurt him.

It's not him. It's not Nix.

He's back on his feet, staring at me, readying himself to

charge me; this time I'm ready for it. He runs at me, but I pretend to be too injured to move. As he gets closer, I check my surroundings and when he is a few feet away I dodge to the left. He slides into a halt, and I jump, grabbing onto his back and wrapping my arms around his throat. I pull back, choking him until his image starts to flicker again.

It's not him. It's not Nix.

His image fades and instead of my brother, I'm holding the neck of a girl with bright red hair. I tighten my grip around her neck and pull her back, cutting her off from oxygen. She doesn't fight me, instead she lets loose a blood curdling scream so loud I lose my grip and fall backwards, covering my ears with my hands. All the stadium lights begin to burst, sending sparks down to the ground around us before covering the field in darkness again. She stops screaming and I uncover my ears, but my eyes need to adjust to the darkness again and I can't see where she is. The earth begins to quake again, a deep rumbling erupts from under my feet, and I stumble, unable to keep balance. The girl with the red hair, I've seen her before, but *where*? I rack my brain, trying to remember, but I can't focus with all the shaking.

The hospital! She was at the hospital.

But that's not the only place I've seen her, I know it. There are two figures at the end of the football field, standing completely still. There were two girls outside of my hospital room. I squint, trying to make out their faces, but it's still too dark out. I start towards them, moving slowly to remain upright, but the quaking makes me stumble and I fall to my knees.

"You should have left him alone."

I look around, no one is near me, but I heard a voice so clear it was like they were right next to me. I bring myself up, but the quaking gets worse, and I fall sideways.

"It's all your fault, their blood is on your hands." The voice tells me.

Get up. You must get up.

I will myself to stand.

Good, now check your surroundings.

I look around, I see no one.

The voice must be coming from somewhere.

I focus my eyes, looking for any movement. Out of the corner of my eye, I can see it. I slight ripple moving past me. I stay frozen in place, but something seems to be traveling in circles around me, it takes the ripple five seconds to reach the front of my face.

"You'll never—" I reach out and grab the girl and slam her to the ground.

"Who are you?" I demand, I get inches away from her face and hold her down by her shoulders with my hands and my knee in her stomach. She stares at me dead in the eyes, no expression. Her red hair has dark black lowlights in it, something I couldn't notice from far away; but it's her eyes that mostly catch my attention. Her eyes shine a brilliant bright blue, like I'm staring at the sky from inside of a bleak house; the same as Zagreus' had when we first met. "Who are you?" I demand again. She just smiles at me.

"You'll never stop us." She sneers, she hasn't struggled under my grip at all.

"What do you mean us?" I ask, pressing my knee into her stomach more.

"You don't have what it takes." She spits. I can hear footsteps approaching to my left, someone is coming, but I can't take my eyes of this girl.

"I asked you a question, answer me."

"And if I don't?" She challenges me, "The clock is ticking." She smiles, "*tick tock, tick tock.*" She mocks.

"Stop messing around and tell me who you are!" I grab her by the shoulders and slam them into the ground. I can hear more footsteps now, but these are coming from the opposite direction as the first set.

"Rose! What are you doing?" Deme calls out.

"You better answer her." The girl sneers.

"No, she's not really here. Now answer me!" I slam her to the ground again, but the girl just laughs in response.

"Rose!" Andrew calls out and I turn towards them, the girl uses this opportunity to flip me over and run. Caught off guard, I reach out to grab at her ankles, but she gets away. I start after her, but someone grabs me from behind.

"Stop, what do you think you're doing?" Zagreus asks me, he has hold of both of my hands behind my back.

"That girl! You're letting her get away!"

"What girl, Rose?" He asks.

"That red-head, I had her pinned but she's getting away. Let go!" I struggle to get free, but his grip tightens around my wrists.

"Come on! Please!" I beg, "Let me go!"

"I'm not letting you go after her alone! Stop struggling and talk to us for a second!" He yells at me, his voice echoing across the empty football field. I hadn't noticed, but the ground stopped shaking. I stop moving and listen for a moment.

"It was her, she's behind all of this. I know she is. The ground was shaking, and she was changing forms or something." I explain to them. "I won't run, I promise. You can let me go." I tell Zagreus. He drops one of my hands but keeps hold of my other so I can turn around and face them.

"Who is this girl?" Deme asks.

"I don't know her name, but she was at the hospital, and I think I know her from somewhere else too. I just can't remember where."

"You said she was a red-head. Was it Jessica?" Andrew asks me.

"Jess might be cold-hearted, but this girl has her beat. No way. Besides, I'd have known it was her." I explain. "Where is Gabby?"

"It's too dangerous for her to be out here, she's just a human. She stayed back with Aphrodite." Deme says.

"Then why are you here?" I ask.

"You're my sister, I couldn't stay back knowing both of my siblings were out here somewhere." She glares, "Did you find Nix?"

"No, I thought I did. But it was just that girl, using his image."

"What does that even mean?" Andrew asks.

"I don't know, she like shape-shifted, she was pretending to be him and Deme to throw me off." I tell him.

"Sounds like you were hallucinating again, but that's just me." Andrew shrugs.

"I wasn't hallucinating!"

"Okay, okay," Deme puts her hand on Andrew's shoulder, "Go back to what she looked like, you said you know who she is?"

"Yeah, she has red hair, but it has these black lowlights in it, and her eyes..." I trail off and look up at Zagreus.

"Wait, you said black lowlights? Was there someone else here? Another girl?" Deme asks.

"I think so, there were two people, but I only ever got close to one. I assumed she was just trying to trick me into thinking there were two of them."

"The wonder twins." Deme says.

"The who?" Andrew asks.

"You wouldn't know." She blows him off and gets close to me, "Do you remember that last day of school, when I was crying in the bathroom, and I told you about those two new girls?" She asks me.

"Oh my god."

"She's one of them!" Deme shouts excitedly, "I knew there was something off about them! Melanie and Mackenzie, those are their names!" Deme is almost bouncing, she's so excited.

Zagreus grips my hand tighter and closes his eyes, "Did you say Melanie and Mackenzie?"

"Yeah why? Do you know them?"

"Yeah, they're my sisters." He says blankly.

"I'm sorry, did I just hear you correctly? The wonder twins are your sisters?" Andrew exclaims, we all look at him, "What? Just trying to stay relevant in the conversation." He shrugs.

"Their real names are Melinoë and Macaria, the Goddess's of nightmares and chaos, and blessed death."

"Which ones which?" Andrew asks, and we all look at him again, "What? It's important, isn't it?"

"Melinoë, is the Goddess of Nightmares and Chaos the one with the red hair, Macaria is the Goddess of blessed death, hers is blue." Zagreus explains, "I should have known they were behind this." He drops my hand and rubs his eyes before realizing he let go of me and quickly grabs my hand again. I roll my eyes at him.

"I thought you said that Hades wasn't behind this?" I ask him.

"He isn't. Melinoë and Macaria are very loyal to him though," He rolls his eyes, "They are his perfect children. They'll do anything and everything to impress him."

"So, what does this mean? What are we supposed to do?" Deme asks, "I mean, they're Gods. We can't just lock them up or whatever."

"No, you guys need to let me deal with them. They are too dangerous."

"I'm not leaving until we find Nix." I state.

"Yeah, and I'm immortal now, so..." Andrew says.

"No, you're not. There are ways to kill a Vampire, especially a new one without any training, and they won't hesitate to do so." Zagreus warns him.

"Deme, you need to go home." I tell her.

"But..."

"No, it's too dangerous. I'll find Nix and bring him home. I'll be fine." I assure her.

"I know better than to argue with you, but Rose, it's dangerous for you too." Zagreus tells me.

"I'm not leaving."

"I figured. But you can't leave my side. Their powers have no effect on me, I can help keep you grounded if they come after you."

"I won't, I'll stay with you the entire time." I assure him, "Take her home Andrew, keep her safe."

"Oh, come on, you guys are really going to leave me out?" He asks.

"I cannot face Gabby without you again. Don't make me." I stare at him dead in the eyes, he challenges me for a second but backs down.

"Fine, I'll keep her safe. I promise." He tells me.

"Tell Aphrodite to train you, she may be annoying, but she does know how to fight. You're going to need to learn." Zagreus tells him and Andrew nods in response. I hug Deme tightly then Andrew as well.

"We'll see you soon, okay?" I tell them both and they nod before heading off towards the parking lot. When they disappear, Zagreus drops my hand and faces me.

"Where to?" He asks.

"I didn't see which way she went, but if you didn't pass her on the way over to me, I'd say she went towards the high school."

"We don't need to guess. Phoenix is an alpha, and your brother, you have a natural connection to him. We just need to access it and you'll be able to track him."

"Why didn't you tell me this sooner?" I ask.

"Oh, like when you were fighting the Vrykolakas, or when you were running off into the night without warning? Rose, you are seriously the most impatient person I've ever met." He smirks.

"Whatever. So, how do I access this *connection*?" I roll my eyes, and he chuckles.

"Close your eyes and concentrate. It would be easier if you were in your wolf form, but you need to conserve your energy in case they come after us again." He tells me.

I close my eyes and take a deep breath in and out, "Okay, now what?"

"You need to relax," I can hear him move around me, he places his hands on my shoulders and rubs them gently, "Think about Nix, and try to picture where he could be."

"I don't see anything."

"That's okay," He whispers in my ear, it takes everything in me not to shudder. "What do you hear?" He asks. I listen, but I can't hear anything but Zagreus breathing loudly into my ears.

"I can't hear anything except your mouth breathing. Back off a bit."

"That's not me," He says, "It's Nix. Now tell me, what do you smell?" I take a deep breath in through my nose.

"It smells like wet, rusty metal. Like a truck in a junkyard after it rains." I explain, "But it also smells like chemicals, like someone was cleaning their house." I hear a ball bouncing and open my eyes. "They're in the gym." I tell him.

"There are two gyms in the direction that they went in."

"Right. But I didn't hear any echoes so they can't be in the dome. They must be in the old gym, its usually open to the public, so maybe they got in because someone forgot to lock the doors." I explain.

"I mean, it's a start. Let's go, and remember, stay—,"

"Stay by your side, I know." I finish his sentence and grab his hand, "Come on."

The old gym is exactly that, old. Since the dome was built, it's now the home for most of the basketball games that take place in town, leaving the old gym neglected and developing its own mildew smell that no amount of cleaning could get rid of. The school likes to let the community use the building for whatever it needs, mostly it gets used as a shelter for displaced locals during wildfire season. But they also tend to leave the building unlocked during summer, so kids have somewhere cooler to play basketball. It's also used for school dances occasionally.

When we get to the entrance of the old gym the entire building is filled with thick, hot steam, almost like someone left all the showers running. The warmth of the building radiates out of the doors as we open them, and the steam begins to dissipate as it pours out of the building. It's hard to make anything out and as we venture deeper into the building Zagreus pulls me closer to him. Together, we make our way onto the basketball court, but as I take a step forward, I trip on something. I would have fallen flat on my face if Zagreus wasn't holding onto me, but I kneel and feel for whatever tripped me. My hand settles on something squishy, I try to use my hand to clear out the steam, hoping I can get a clearer look at what this is. I reach out again and grab a hold of it, realizing that what I'm grabbing onto is wet denim, I scurry backwards towards Zagreus.

"It's a person." I tell him and he ushers me behind him, still holding my hand and reaches down toward the person. A hand comes out of nowhere and latches onto his forearm, pulling him down closer to them.

"Don't go down there." It's just a kid, and he sounds exhausted, "It's a trap." He says before letting go of Zagreus and laying back down on the basketball court again. Zagreus stands up and gets close to me.

"Is there a basement?" He whispers.

"Not really, the locker rooms are down a couple flights of stairs though." I whisper back, he nods and tugs on my hand to keep following him. We follow the length of the wall until we find the stairwell that leads down to the locker rooms. The steam is unbelievably thick here and my skin is already covered in a layer of moisture as we continue down the steps. My foot slips and I start to fall down the stairs, but Zagreus still has a hold on my hand and grabs me before I start tumbling down.

"You good?" He asks.

"Yeah, thanks." I nod and we continue down the stairs. This time I'm aware that the ground is building a thick layer of water on it and try to watch my step. I can't help but think about how all this moisture can't be good for the old building. If Zagreus' sisters cause another quake, the entire building could be compromised and collapse on top of us. Almost as if they were listening to my thoughts, the building begins to shake. Zagreus drops my hand and grabs onto the railing. I can hear the building crack and crumble around us, it knocks me backwards on the stairs.

"Rose!" Zagreus calls out, "Find something to hold onto!" I look around, but the steam and dust are clouding my vision. I go back up a few steps and grab onto the railing at the same time the roof begins to cave in on itself. "Rose, get out of here!" Zagreus calls out to me again.

"What about you?" I call back.

"I'll be fine, just get somewhere safe!" He tells me, the roof completely caves in on us as I scramble up the stairs. The building stops shaking, I try to clear the air in front of me by waving my hands in front of my face. Zagreus and I have been cut off from each other. A pile of wood and debris blocks the stairwell. He's stuck down there. "Rose. Rose, can you hear me?" He calls out his voice muffled by the debris.

"Yeah, are you okay?" I ask.

"I'm fine. Look, just get out of here. I'll find Nix and portal out of here. Get out of here, I'll meet you at your house. Okay?"

"Promise me." I tell him.

"What?" He asks.

"Promise me that you'll be okay."

"I promise, now go. It's too dangerous for both of us to stay in this spot." I nod even though he can't see me and begin to ascend the stairs on my hands and knees.

At the top of the stairs, I pull myself up onto my feet and take a good look around. The ceiling has a major crack, running from one end of the building to the other, the steam filters through it, escaping out of the building. The basketball hoop has fallen from the ceiling and shattered, broken glass litters the court. The boy from earlier is still in the building, kneeling over another person. I make my way over to them, wary of another quake. Both boys have blood on their clothes.

"What are you still doing here?" I ask them.

"He can't walk. She broke his leg." The boy from earlier tells me, he has dark brown hair and a bloody wound above his left eye that's pooling into his eye-socket. I look at the other boy, he's dirty blonde and olive skinned but doesn't appear to have any other wounds aside from his leg. I get closer to the boy on the ground and begin to pull his pant leg up, he shouts in pain.

"Shh. It's okay, I just want to look at it." I tell him and his head drops back to the floor. "You," I say to the brunette, "Grab hold of his hand, and let him squeeze as hard as he needs to." He does as I ask, and I quickly try to pull the hem of his jeans over his shin. The boy groans in pain and I almost faint at the sight of his leg; its worse than I thought. His shinbone is split and protruding from his skin. Blood pools around his legs and covers my hands. I need to think quickly or he's going to lose too much blood. There's a shard of glass next to me, I rip the hem of my shirt and use the cloth to wrap around the bottom of the shard. With my make-shift knife, I begin sawing at the boys' jeans just above his knee. Once I make the final cut through the denim, I beckon for the brunette to take off his shirt and hand it to me. He does without hesitation, and I rip the hem of his shirt off and hand it back to him, "Tie that around your head to cover the wound on your forehead." I tell him as I take the remainder of the shirt and tie it above the knee of the boys broken leg. I look around for a stick or something and find a small piece of piping still connected to the fire sprinkler that fell from the roof. I hit the sprinkler on the ground until it falls off and tie the pipe into the fabric before twisting it tighter. He whimpers as the fabric tightens around his leg, but I ignore his cries and tie the pipe into place, carefully ensuring that the pipe can't move.

"How do you know how to do that?" The brunette asks me.

"My best friend broke his ankle falling off a jungle gym once, the bone was coming out through his skin and wouldn't stop bleeding. His dad is in the military, and he did this to him when the ambulance took too long to get there. I wasn't sure I remembered how until now though." I explain.

"You're Rose, aren't you?" The brunette asks now.

"Yeah, how do you know me?" I ask him.

"You saved us, my brother and I." He motions towards the boy on the floor, "That's my brother, Ty. I'm Alex."

"You guys are wolves." I deduce and Alex nods in response. "Were you with Nix? Where is he?" I ask.

He looks towards the staircase that I just came from, "He's down there still, we got separated, Ty got hurt and I needed to protect him. He's just a kid, barely fourteen, I told him not to come but he wouldn't listen." He explains.

"We need to get him out of here, okay? You can walk, right?" I ask and Alex nods. I stand up, I hold my hand out to help him up, but he declines. "Here's what we're gonna do, okay?" I go around to Ty's head, "I'll lift him from here, but you need to grab hold of his hands and pull him up from there. Ty don't try to use your broken leg. Just relax." We get into position and Alex makes eye contact with me, "On the count of three, okay?" I say but I hold up two fingers behind Ty's head to signal to Alex that we're going to do it early.

"One..." I pause, and make direct eye contact with Alex, "Two..." We both lift Ty up, Alex wraps Ty in a hug while I make sure his leg isn't losing too much blood and that the tourniquet is still in place. "Alright, Lets go." I tell them. Alex puts one of Ty's arms around his shoulders while I place his other arm around mine. The pace we move at is slow, but at least we're moving away from this death trap. I can only hope that Zagreus has found Nix and they're both okay. We head for the same doors that Zagreus and I came through, it'll give us a clear path to the parking lot where I can keep an eye on them and try to flag down some help.

When we get to the doors, the earth begins to quake again. Alex and I stand our ground, planting our feet firmly and trying to remain balanced so we don't drop his brother. I can hear footsteps behind us, loud clicking, like whoever it is, is wearing heels.

"Turn into a wolf, grab your brother and get out of here." I tell Alex.

"What about you?" He asks.

"Don't worry about me, get to the parking lot and across the street, pound on as many doors as it takes to get someone to call an ambulance for him." I explain.

"I don't... I don't know if I can turn right now." He tells me.

"You have to." I tell him and take his brothers weight onto me. I watch as Alex's body begins to crack and mangle into half man, half wolf. It looks painful, but I know that he doesn't feel much pain because he doesn't make a sound. When he's done, I help Ty hobble over to him. Alex picks him up and I run over to the doors and prop them open for them. "Go, get him help and don't look back." I say before I take off back into the gymnasium.

I walk to the center of the court; the dust is beginning to settle and the steam evaporating thanks to the crack in the ceiling. I look around for either of Zagreus' sisters, but I don't see them.

"It's just you and me now!" I shout, "Come out and face me!" I listen quietly. Water drops from the ceiling, splashing gently on the ground.

"You think you can take me twice?" A girl's voice laughs. I follow the sound of her voice to the top of the bleachers. Melinoë stands tall and proud, a smirk on her face. Her hands are on her hips, and she doesn't appear to have a scratch on her from our fight earlier.

"What do you want from me?" I ask her.

"I don't want anything from *you*." She spits.

"Then why go through all of this? Why lead my brother here?"

"I'm just simply fixing my brother's mess. If you pay for it in the process, then so be it." A wicked grin spreads across her face.

"Is that what this is about? Zagreus?"

"No, it's about keeping you creatures in line." She takes a step down, "You think you're so powerful, taking down the thousand-year-old plan that my father put into place. You are nothing but a filthy mutt who should've been put down with the dogs. We welcomed you into our home and you made a fool out of my parents. You will not make a fool out of *me*." Each time she steps down the bleachers, the earth shakes but I remain balanced. "You turned my brother into a love-sick fool, converted him to your side when he should be standing among the Gods. You made Aphrodite fall from grace, reduce herself to that of a human." She reaches the bottom step and stops. "You need to be punished."

8

No Mercy

Dust rains down from the ceiling as the earth begins to quake and distort around me. Melinoë reaches her arms out, spreading them apart before pulling them back in and clapping her hands together. As she does this, the walls pull in close around me, leaving me in what seems like a tunnel; a tunnel that only leads to her. She smiles wickedly, throws her hair behind her shoulder, and begins to shift her appearance. Melinoë's skin changes color first, half of her body becoming dark as a moonless night, the other as luminous as a supermoon. Her hair does the same, splitting right down the middle, one side bright white, the other a deep black. I can't move, something about her appearance causes my hair to stand on end, I can't help but feel frightened, even though she hasn't done anything yet. When she's done, she takes another step down, we're on the same level now.

She's trying to intimidate you. Don't fall for it.

I don't move an inch, not wanting to show her my fear, but I've never fought a Goddess before. She can't die, and I most likely won't be able to hurt her. I should've run when I had the chance to. I hope Alex was able to get his brother to help. I hope Nix is okay, and Zagreus.

The walls aren't real, it's just a hallucination.

Melinoë begins to move toward me, slow and steady, more confident of herself than I've ever been. It feels like the walls are moving closer to me, but it isn't real. She is the Goddess of Nightmares and Chaos, she is manipulating my vision somehow, turning reality into a nightmare.

I take a deep breath, center my point of gravity, and begin to transform into a wolf. Melinoë uses this to her advantage and begins to run at full speed towards me, barely giving me enough time to dodge to the right as she attempts to grab me. She shrieks and flips around to face me, I lean down, readying myself to pounce on her. She runs at me in full force again, but I don't back down, instead I throw myself into her, throwing her off balance and onto her back. I attempt to pin her, but she punches my stomach, *hard*. I yelp and fall to her side. Melinoë lunges for me, reaching out to wrap her arms around my neck but I bite into her forearm and shake my head, digging my fangs into her skin until I feel bone. Blood pours from her wounds, filling my mouth and spilling onto the ground. She screams out in agony and attempts to pull away, shaking and throwing her arms around wildly. This only causes more damage to her arm; I can feel my teeth ripping away at her skin and muscle tissue. She grabs the back of my neck and pulls me off her before throwing me halfway across the room; she's stronger than she looks.

I skid across the floor, my claws digging into the wood to slow me down.

I hurt her enough to break whatever spell she was doing to the gymnasium. The walls are back where they should be, I was right, it was all a hallucination. Dust particles are floating through the air, across from me I can barely make out Melinoë's figure. She's probably already healed her arm, and I'm still struggling to breathe steadily. I attempt to stand, but in the process, I realize I'm running on fumes. My legs are shaking, I've probably broken a few ribs, and I feel like I'm going to throw up, but I stay standing. She's going to come for me again, any second, and I have to be ready for her.

The ground quakes, dust and debris begin to rain down, the crack in the ceiling becoming larger and larger. I ready myself for her attack, bracing for impact from any direction. She hits me from the left and together we tumble across the floor. A large piece of shingling lands next to us and I can hear pipes begin to burst around us, showering us with water. She's clutching my fur, refusing to let go, but every time she thinks she has me pinned, I flip her over onto her back. I manage to claw at her arm that I bit earlier, she cries in pain and shoves me off her. The ground is becoming slick as the burst pipes continue to spew water. My wet fur begins to weigh me down. I *need* to get out of here.

I bolt for the exit, but every turn I make, Melinoë is right on top of me, countering my every move. I jump over a pile of fallen roof and slip as I hit the slick wooden court, sliding into a wall. I can't help but return to my human form, I'm exhausted from the fight and my injuries. In the pale moonlight I check myself over quickly. My head is bleeding from somewhere, there is also dried blood on my mouth, although I don't know if it is mine or Melinoë's. I have *definitely* broken more than a few ribs, and the scars on my side are throbbing. If I'm not careful, I'm going to pass out. I really need to get out of here.

Melinoë seems to have slowed down, I'm not sure, but the quakes seem less powerful, and I can hear a limp in her footsteps. I feel around for a weapon, anything I can use to protect myself. There are chunks of plaster, pieces of roofing that have fallen, before finally my hand settles on a metal rod of some sort and I pick it up, weighing it in my hands. Using the wall, I begin to rise. I steady myself, my legs still shaking. Melinoë's footsteps draw nearer, I can make out her figure, limping towards me at a slow pace. Each step she takes sends a wave of water towards me, the room now almost a foot deep in water, I can hear the water running down the steps to the locker room, I hope Zagreus and Nix got out before it started flooding. I hold the metal rod tightly behind my back, waiting for the right moment to pull it out. I can't kill a God, but I can make her wish she was dead. I muster up every ounce of energy that I have left and begin to run at a full sprint towards Melinoë. A few steps away from her, I pull the metal rod out, grip it tightly in both of my hands and aim for her head.

I make contact with Melinoë's head, and she drops to the ground, there is a small splash as her body hits a pile of debris on the soaked basketball court and I drop down on her. Her head is resting on a wooden plank, keeping her above the water but the rest of her body is almost completely submerged. I use my knees to pin down her shoulders before taking the metal rod and stabbing it through her right shoulder. I use all my body weight to push the rod down into her body. Ignoring her blood curdling screams, I push the rod down deeper, feeling her bones shift in the process. Blood pours out from the wound, mixing with the water on the ground, but I still push harder, until the metal rod hits the floor.

"Why are you here?" I demand.

She tries to talk but spits up blood first. "I told...told you," She struggles, but I twist the rod and she wince's again, "To...punish...you."

"You are the ones who kidnapped all those wolves, your mother took my best friend and turned him into that monster. Haven't I been punished enough?" I ask her.

"Not... we didn't do that." She says spitting up more blood and trying to control her breathing.

"What do you mean?"

"He did that to himself." Her eyes are narrow, blood trails down her mouth. "You destroyed my family."

"*I* didn't do anything. That was all you." I tell her.

"You can't kill me." She whispers.

"No, but I can make you wish that I could." I twist the metal rod around and she screams again before I place my hands around her neck. "Which would you prefer?" I ask, "Buried so deep in the woods that no one will ever find you, or chopped up into little pieces that are spread throughout the world, that no one will ever be able to put you back together again?"

"You wouldn't." She spits.

"You have been terrorizing me for months." I tell her, "Making me feel like I was crazy, killing innocent people in this town, and you have been trying to kill me all night, you think I'm just going to let you walk out of here?" I laugh, "Guess again." I tighten my grip around her throat. She doesn't say anything, just stares at me. Her eyes narrow, almost daring me to do it.

The full moonlight floods in through the hole in the ceiling, filling the room with its light. I keep my eyes on Melinoë. She doesn't gasp for air or make any sound, doesn't move an inch as my hands close around her neck.

"Please," she says softly and closes her eyes. "I'm begging you to stop."

I freeze. Is she asking me not to kill her? Is this a trick? If I let go of her, pull out the metal rod, is she just going to let you go? No, she is going to kill me. She is a monster that needs to be destroyed.

It takes a monster to kill a monster.

Am I a monster? I look at my hands, still at her throat, then at the metal rod extruding from her shoulder, still bleeding. Her blood is everywhere, clouding the water around us, covering my hands and her body.

I let go of her neck.

"Rose!" I hear a muffled voice call out. I stand up and look down at Melinoë. She isn't moving, but her eyes examine me. I can hear footsteps splashing as they close in on us.

"Don't make me regret this." I tell Melinoë, giving her one last look before I step away from her and straight into the arms of Zagreus. I collapse into him, letting my arms wrap around his warm body, not giving in to my thoughts that this may be too much. In this moment, I don't care about anyone else.

"Rose, what... are you okay?" He asks me as tears

pour from my eyes, trailing down my cheeks. He runs his hand through my bloodstained hair and caresses my head. I bury my face in his chest. "It's okay." He shushes me, "You're going to be okay." He whispers.

"I'm sorry-"

"Don't be." He tells me. He bends at the knee and scoops me up into his arms. As he carries me to the exit, I take one last look at Melinoë, laying in a pool of her own blood. She turns her head, burying half of it in water as she does so, we make eye contact just before Zagreus walks through the doors. Through the crack of the doors, just before they close, Melinoë looks up, her face illuminated in the moonlight, and she closes her eyes.

"Rose!" Nix jumps out of Gabby's car and runs over to Zagreus and I. "Thank god you're okay, I don't know what I'd do if you weren't." Zagreus carefully tips me down onto my feet and I wrap my brother in a hug.

"What were you thinking?" I ask him, not really looking for an answer.

"I don't know, it was a trap, and I didn't even get a punch in before she grabbed me." Nix explains, he lets go and holds my shoulders in his hands, "You look terrible, we need to get you home."

"I'm fine." I assure him, even though my whole body feels like it's on fire. "Where are Alex and Ty? Did they get out of here?"

"The two wolves that came after me?" Nix asks, I nod. "They're fine, we passed an ambulance on the way here."

"How do you know it was them?" I ask, wanting to be sure.

"Trust me, it was them." He looks at me in the eyes and I realize that I believe him.

"Why did you guys come back?" I ask, looking between the pair. Nix looks at Zagreus to answer.

"When I got to Nix, Macaria was just sitting there. She didn't want to fight. She let me unchain him." He starts. So, that's where the other sister was, guarding their captive. "Macaria is gentle, she doesn't like to hurt people, but she is naïve and was tricked by our sister that this was the right thing to do. You must understand, Rose, Macaria is very much on our side." Zagreus explains to me. I look at Nix, they are hiding something from me, but I don't know what, until Nix steps aside. Macaria is sitting in the back of Gabby's car. She isn't looking at us, but instead at her hands, some sort of bug crawls across her fingers. "I couldn't leave her down there, Melinoë was going to get her exiled. We took a portal back to your house and when Deme realized we weren't with you, she made us come back. We decided to take the car in case Melinoë's quakes destroyed the portal; it was close enough the first time." Zagreus continues, although I don't really pay attention to what he is saying. From this close, Macaria doesn't look like a teenager at all. She looks like a child, barely thirteen years old. Her pale skin and pastel blue hair glows in the shadows of the car. I can't help but feel sorry for her.

"It's fine." I say, cutting off Zagreus from whatever he was saying. "Forget about Macaria, you need to get Melinoë before she heals herself."

"Rose, Melinoë doesn't heal like the rest of us. She was born in the mouth of the river Cocytus; she needs those waters to heal." He tells me, "You stabbed her with a metal pole, she isn't going anywhere."

"You WHAT?" Nix exclaims, his eyes wide. "Dang, Rose. Remind me not to hit you again." He chuckles. But I'm barely paying attention so him. I *could* have killed Melinoë. I mean, Hades probably would have resurrected her, but that was still murder in my book.

Zagreus puts a hand on my shoulder and gets close to me, "Ignore him." He whispers. "You need to get some rest. Let's get you home." He tells me, placing his hand on my back.

I shake my head, "Not until we take care of Melinoë." I tell him.

"Rose I told you, she can't heal." He sighs.

"We can't let her die."

"I'm sorry, did I just hear you correctly?" Nix presses a finger to his temple, "This girl has been trying to kill you all night and has been using an undead army to terrorize the town, and you want to *save* her."

"Yes." I state.

Nix drops his hands to his side, "You are unbelievable, Rose." He sighs, "Unbelievable."

"The Cocytus River is in the Underworld. I'll have to create a portal to take her there. But if she dies, Hades will resurrect her, she will live no matter what." Zagreus explains.

"We are going to get her to that river, Zagreus." I tell him.

He shakes his head, "I can't believe this, but okay. Let's

go get her." he sighs. I hold my hand out for him to take and he does, intertwining his fingers with mine.

Back inside the old gym, everything has settled. The water is barely dripping from the pipes, and all the dust has settled onto the water. It ripples away from us as we approach Melinoë. She still isn't moving, and now that my vision is clear, I realize that the bright white half of her body has dimmed to reveal an ethereal skeleton; It was her bones that were glowing. The arm that I had bitten into, the dark skin that is so dark it's like I'm looking at a hole in the ground, is shredded, revealing the same glowing bones. I go to pull out the metal rod sticking out of her shoulder, but Zagreus stops me.

"She could bleed out, leave it until we get there." He tells me and I nod. "I can't create the portal in here, the building is unstable and could collapse around us if I do. We need to get her out of here." He speaks. He goes to her bends down, whispers something to her that I don't understand, and lifts her up. She looks like a sleeping child being carried up to bed.

We head back outside to the parking lot, and Zagreus places her body on the ground gently. She's awake, I can see her eyes moving, but Melinoë hasn't spoken a word to us. Nix is back in the car, sitting in the front seat with the door propped open.

"Mac, let's go." Zagreus calls out and Macaria gets out of the car and approaches us. She looks down at her sister and back up at me but doesn't say a word. "Phoenix, go home. Tell everyone we will be back soon. I'll get some food for Andrew while were down there."

"You got it." Nix replies walking around to the driver's

seat. He salutes us before he drives off. Zagreus walks a few feet away from us, leaving me with his two sisters. Macaria doesn't look at me nor Melinoë, she stares straight down at the ground not making a sound. Macaria is probably stronger than she lets on, but I don't know anything about her other than her being the Goddess of "Blessed Death" whatever that means.

Zagreus kneels, claps his hands together and places both of his palms against the asphalt. The earth rumbles a bit, nothing like the quakes Melinoë was able to produce, and splits open. A five-foot hole of darkness opens in the parking lot. Zagreus picks Melinoë back up and walks to the edge.

"Mac, you first, then Rose, I'll follow you guys." He tells us, Macaria jumps a little and walks over to the hole. She steps into the hole without thinking twice about it and disappears. "Okay, your turn." Zagreus cocks his head towards me, beckoning me to step into the hole.

"Is it safe?" I ask, he chuckles in response.

"Of course, it is, just go. I'm right behind you." He assures me. I nod, take a deep breath, and let myself fall into the dark pit.

It takes less than one second for me to land in the underworld. I'm in a familiar place. Illuminated by hundreds of glowing crystals, is the turquoise river with the waterfall. I look around, sure enough the staircase we descended all those months ago is behind me. A moment later Zagreus is standing next to me, Melinoë in his arms. Macaria is bent down, examining something in the grass, she looks up at Zagreus and he smiles at her.

"Rose, don't touch the water." He tells me and heads

down to the water's edge. I follow behind him, while Macaria follows behind silently. Zagreus takes a step into the water, and it begins to rise, like hands reaching out to grab him and wrapping around his legs. He ignores this though and continues to wade deeper into the water. The current picks up, moving quickly and splashing so hard I take a step back, afraid to get hit by the droplets. Carefully, Zagreus begins to lower Melinoë into the water, and I might be imagining it, but it sounds like the river is crying. When she is neck deep in the water, Zagreus lets go of her, pulls the metal rod from her shoulder and lets the current take her away.

I take a step forward, "What are you—"

"Stay back!" Zagreus warns as he steps out of the river and I freeze in place, "She'll be fine." The water completely engulfs her and begins to glow as it carries her downstream. I watch her body float away until I can't see it anymore. Zagreus puts an arm around me, "Let's get Macaria home, grab some food for Andrew and get you home." He squeezes my shoulder and heads towards the hidden staircase next to the waterfall.

After the ferry ride across the river, we make our way to Cerberus. We hadn't come this way last time we were here and being this close to the massive dog with three heads makes me feel uneasy. Hundreds of spirits are lined up in front of him, they glow brightly in the darkness, slowly moving towards the big iron gates Cerberus guards. This is where we leave Macaria. She skips over to the spirits, welcoming each one of them to the afterlife on her way, and passes through the gates.

"Macaria, is the Goddess of Blessed Death, she helps

guide the souls to their final resting place." Zagreus explains. I can't help but picture my mother, walking through the gates and holding the hand of a girl barely older than myself at the time she passed. I wonder what my mother must have thought of her. Zagreus tugs on my sleeve and I follow him, around the line of souls and through the hidden gate we used the first time we were here, and onto the boat where we have to row ourselves.

This time around, Zagreus avoids having to go to the crystal palace. Although I'm not sure if he's doing it for my sake or his so that he doesn't have to see his parents; either way I'm okay with this. We work our way around the palace, taking various paths, until we end up right next to a tiny farm behind the castle. Apparently, agriculture in the Underworld is more prominent than I originally thought. There are more animals than I imagined, although they are all a dark midnight black in color. Zagreus goes through the gate, beckons me to follow him and closes it behind us. A large man walks out of the stable and turns to us, squints, and sighs before waving us over.

"Was wonderin' when you'd show." He says, his voice low and his speech drawn out. He's wearing overalls, a straw hat and his white shirt is covered in mud, sweat stains and what looks like dried blood. We follow him back into the stable and although I don't see any animals, it smells like them; I force myself to breathe through my mouth to avoid the smell, but it only makes it worse. The man leads us into a back room filled with machinery and over to an area with multiple refrigerators. He opens one of them, grabs a few metal canisters and hands them directly to Zagreus. "Should last a while." He grunts, Zagreus nods at him.

"Appreciate it Menoites." Zagreus thanks him and we head back out. When we get out of earshot of the man, Zagreus hands me one of the cannisters. "Menoites is a man of few words, but he always delivers, mom is pretty fond of him too." He tells me as we cross through the gate again. "Let's get out of here." He smiles and hands me the rest of the cannisters, I can feel liquid moving around in them as I try to balance them in my hands. Zagreus opens a portal on the ground, takes the cannisters back from me and grabs my free hand. Together we step down into the portal and disappear into darkness.

9

Let the Flames Begin

"I think I'm going to be sick." Deme gags. Andrew is chugging down the contents of one of the metal cannisters that Zagreus and I brought back from the underworld. I don't think I've ever seen him drink anything so fast, and he doesn't waste a single drop of it either.

"Dude, seriously, this has to last a minute." Zagreus rolls his eyes; Andrew doesn't even acknowledge him.

"He didn't have boundaries with food before, kid would eat a mountain of mom's pancakes for breakfast and still be hungry. What did you expect?" Nix asks as he watches Andrew in disgusted delight.

Deme gags again, "It's like watching those pimple popping videos only ten times worse." We only made it a few feet into the house before Andrew knew that we had food for him, it was like he had a sixth sense for the stuff. We didn't even get a chance to talk about anything that happened before Andrew was chugging away. Zagreus put the rest of the containers into the fridge, but I'm considering hiding them in the fridge in the basement with Aph.

While watching my best friend chug a bottle of blood is a blast, I excuse myself to take a shower, suddenly aware that I smell terrible and haven't showered in days. My injuries are worse than I thought. There is massive bruising around my neck and shoulders, along with dried blood in my hair and on my throat. The scars on my side are almost completely gone, but they are covered in deep purple bruises along with the rest of my chest.

But there are also bruises you can't see.

I almost killed someone, and in the moment, I wanted to.

I almost killed a living being and it shouldn't matter that she was trying to kill me first, and it doesn't. It's the same thing. It takes a monster to kill a monster. And it would have been easy. It would have been the easiest thing to do in the moment. It would have made me no better than Tyler, who is sitting in jail for hurting me, for hurting another girl after me, and who knows how many before me. I feel a lump rise in my throat, but I force back my tears and shake my head. I didn't kill her, I wouldn't. I can't let myself believe that I would. In the warm running water, I scrub the dried blood off myself, rinse it from my hair, and watch it swirl down the drain. Melinoë will be okay, Zagreus told me she would be. I have to hold out hope that someday, she might forgive me for what I've done.

I dress quickly in an oversized t-shirt and running shorts, but before heading out the door I stop. I walk over to my bed and lift the pillow, where the small leather bracelet Zagreus had given me, sits. I turn it over in my hands, examining the moonstone and silver wolf before slipping it over my hand to rest on my wrist.

Downstairs, my dad is coming through the front door. Behind him, is an older man, who I vaguely remember from down in the Underworld. Dad motions for me to follow him and the three of us go to the living room where everyone else is waiting for us. I take a seat on the couch, in between Zagreus and Deme, Nix and Andrew are sitting on the floor, while Aph takes her place in a recliner and my dad, and the old man sit on the other couch. Gabby isn't here, I'm wondering if she went home or if my dad told her to sit this one out while I was in the shower.

"I heard you all had an eventful night." Dad starts, "Arthur and I just left the hospital, Alex is fine, and Ty is recovering from surgery."

"He didn't lose—" I start asking.

"He had to get a few rods in his leg, he broke a few bones, but he's lucky you got him out of there." Dad looks at me, I can tell he is genuinely grateful.

"Thank you, for making sure he's okay." Nix says, I look over at him and I can tell something is wrong with him, but I can't quite make out what it is.

"Anyway, this thing with the Vrykolakas is over, right?" My dad asks Zagreus.

"On behalf of my siblings, I apologize for the stress this has been for all of you. Melinoë and Macaria will not be a problem anymore." Zagreus tells him, Aphrodite snorts.

"Melinoë is unruly, what makes you so sure she won't be a

further problem?" Aph asks him. Zagreus looks at me, Nix and him are the only ones that know what I did to her, that I almost killed a God.

"You're just going to have to trust me." Zagreus tells her, although she doesn't look like she believes him.

"I almost killed her." I pipe up, every single eye in the room looks to me.

"What do you mean?" Deme asks.

"I didn't know..." I start, unable to find the words that go next.

"Melinoë is unlike the rest of the Gods, given the circumstances of her birth, she cannot heal like Aphrodite, and I can. Rose didn't know this and due to the number of injuries Melinoë sustained, it is likely she wouldn't have made it if we didn't take her back to the Underworld." Zagreus explains to the room.

"She stabbed her with a metal rod." Nix adds, my dad looks at me funny.

"Melinoë will be out for the count for a while to fully heal. Like I said, we don't need to worry about her." Zagreus finishes.

"Well then," My dad clears his throat, "I guess we can begin the extermination of the remaining Vrykolakas." He turns to the man sitting next to him. "We should gather the others and prepare them."

"What do you mean prepare the others?" Nix asks.

"It seems, that more of the wolves have come to help when they thought you were in danger. They are currently at one of the housing developments waiting for word on what we do next." Dad explains. "Son, you will need to be a part of this. It is time you step up to the role of their Alpha and I will help guide you."

"It's about time." Nix stands, a little taller than normal, his hands are clenched by his sides and his glare is locked onto our father. Dad motions to confront this sudden tension when I swear Nix can hear my internal pleas to calm down. "Let's go kick some zombie butt." Nix says smiling at the rest of the room putting everyone back at ease.

The house is filled with wolves by the end of the night. It took a few trips to get them all over to the house, but by sunset, it is standing room only. It's hard to believe that this many wolves were displaced after being trapped in the Underworld, and kind of sad too. The ages of the wolves vary, although it seems like Alex and Ty were the youngest of the wolves that returned. The oldest of the wolves is a man named Arthur who is—if I had to guess—around seventy years old. I didn't get the opportunity to sit and listen to a lot of their stories, but Arthur stuck out. Arthur's wife was sick, she had some kind of cancer, I'm not sure which, but she was diagnosed before Arthur was taken to the Underworld. After he was taken, the worry worsened her illness. As soon as she came to the conclusion she would never see her beloved again, she became terminal. He'd been on the missing persons list for four years and was presumed dead. Arthur lost everything because of Hades. His home, his job, and most importantly his wife, were all gone when he came back. He didn't have any other choice but to come to Paradise.

Arthur is also the only wolf who wasn't extremely mad at Zagreus. Of course, when they walked in and saw the man who kidnapped them, most of their reactions were exactly what you'd think they would be; but not Arthur. Arthur walked up to Zagreus and shook his hand. Zagreus of course, not knowing how to react to this, took it upon himself to make amends with everyone. I'd seen him shake hands with at least half of the men in the room by now, apologizing to each one individually before moving onto the next. Dad and Nix are in the kitchen, sitting at the table discussing what their moves are going to be. You'd think since I'm the only one here that has actually gone up against the Vry that they would want some input on how to hunt them, but the look on dad's face when I tried to join in on the discussion was enough to make me run with my tail between my legs.

I'm sitting on the staircase, trying to listen in on the game plan, but there is so much noise in the room that it's hard to focus on what they are saying. Deme sits next to me on the stairs and squeezes my knee.

"How are you feeling?" She asks.

"Alright, I guess." I tell her.

"Why do you guess?"

"Just wish I could be more helpful, sucks to be on the sidelines." I explain.

"I think it's a good thing you're on the sidelines for now." She tells me, "You've had almost no time to rest. Between leaving the hospital and fighting Melinoë, you haven't slept at all." She explains.

"Yeah, it's been a pretty long night." I sigh. "They aren't going to let me help at all, are they?" I ask.

"No." Deme says flatly, "And Zagreus is meant to be watching you, so if you even try to leave." She drags her finger across her throat, and I chuckle at her.

"Honestly, I could use a break." I sigh, "it feels like it's been weeks since I got a decent night's sleep. Did we even eat anything today?" I ask her.

"I think watching Andrew chug a full bottle of blood ruined all of our appetites." She frowns. Dad and Nix walk through the archway to the kitchen.

"Listen up," Dad clears his throat, "We want you all to get into groups of three, these things tend to travel in packs, and it is important that you make sure to stake them, it's the only way to put them down for good."

"It doesn't need to be special wood either, as long as its wood, it'll work." Nix adds.

"If you find a group of them, call for back up. We don't want to get outnumbered and end up dead." Dad looks around, "I have a map of the town on the kitchen table, get into your groups and we'll start assigning districts for each of you." The men mumble amongst themselves but listen to my father. They quickly manage to break into groups of three and follow my dad and Nix into the kitchen, before leaving without a word. The house slowly begins to quiet down as they all disappear outside in the night. Dad, Arthur, and Nix are the last to leave after making me swear that I wouldn't attempt to go after them. Eventually, it's just Deme, Zagreus, Andrew, and I left in the house by ourselves.

Deme puts on some random show on tv while Zagreus checks the perimeter of the house to make sure none of the Vry are around, leaving Andrew and I in the kitchen cooking up something for everyone to eat.

"Where'd Gabby and Aph go?" I ask, looking through the refrigerator for something I can make.

"Back to Gabby's. Her mom was going to be coming back

from her shift at the hospital and Gabby didn't want her to freak when she realized she wasn't home. Aph went with her for protection." Andrew explains.

I pull out some leftover spaghetti, open the lid and smell the sauce. I'm not sure how long it's been in there, but it still smells good, so I transfer it into a pot and put it on the stove along with some water to boil for the noodles. "Spaghetti will have to do." I say, sitting down at the table with Andrew.

"I wonder if I can still eat real food." Andrew says.

"I'm surprised you haven't tried." I laugh and he glares at me for a moment.

"I just haven't thought about it, I don't really feel hungry anymore." He tells me.

"That has to be the only drastic change about you then." I joke, but Andrew doesn't laugh. He just looks down at the table. "You good?" I ask him.

He fiddles with his hands and doesn't meet my eyes, "Yeah, I mean... it's just weird being back."

"How do you mean?"

"I never expected to be back home, never expected to see you, or Gabby, or anyone every again. I thought I was stuck down there."

"I'm sorry we left you down there." I tell him, he finally looks up at me.

"Don't be, I told you to leave, and they weren't going to let me go without a fight. The only reason they let me go in the first place is because I turned into this." He points at his teeth, which I'm just now noticing that his canines look sharper than they used to. There isn't much different about Andrew, he mostly looks the exact same as I left him. Aside from his newly sharper teeth, no one would even be able to tell he was a vampire.

"Do you feel any different?" I ask him.

"Loads." He exaggerates, "Honestly, I feel like I could run a marathon, or climb the tallest mountain in a day. Other than that, I don't feel any different at all." He explains.

"I missed you." I tell him.

"I missed you too." He smiles. The pot of water begins to boil, and I get up to add the noodles and stir the sauce, so it doesn't burn.

We spend the next few hours doing absolutely nothing. Zagreus comes and goes as he maintains the perimeter of the house, but we don't hear back from anyone on how the extermination of the Vry is going and I'm starting to get antsy. Deme went to bed hours ago and even though I'm not sure how, Andrew is sleeping on the couch. I head up to my room around midnight, change into my pajamas and crawl into bed.

I wake up to a light tapping on my bedroom door. It is still dark in my room, but I can see the moon beginning to sink over the mountains out my bedroom window. My eyes feel heavy, and I'm tempted to go back to sleep but instead I throw the blankets off me and open my bedroom door.

"Hey." Zagreus whispers.

"Hey." I reply sleepily, "Is everything okay?"

"Yeah, I was just checking on you. Making sure you're okay." He shifts back and forth on his feet, and he isn't looking at me.

"Are you sure you're alright?"

"Yeah." He smiles, "Go back to bed. I'll wake you if anything changes."

"Okay, Thank you." I smile. We both linger for a moment; I stare into his crystal blue eyes, and he stares into mine. Neither of us saying anything. In the darkness, in the shadows of the moonlight, I am reminded how beautiful he is. It has been a long time since I let myself feel this way, to look at Zagreus and not be angry with him. He takes a step forward, closing in on the little space between us. He leans in, so carefully. Breathing and not breathing. My heart is pounding in my chest, he is close, so close, and I can't feel my legs anymore. I can't feel my fingers or the cold air in the room. All I can feel is him, filling in the empty spaces between us.

He kisses me, without warning and without permission. His lips gently caress my own, soft skin on softer skin. The rush is like plunging from the highest point of a rollercoaster: sheer exhilaration, breathlessness, half a heart attack. His embrace tightens around me, one hand at my neck, the other around the small of my back. Our bodies fit together like a puzzle piece, neither one of us complete without the other. I make a sound I didn't know was possible, and I didn't mean it to be encouraging, but Zagreus kisses me deeper. The warmth of his body envelopes me and I can feel his heart beating just as fast as mine.

A blood curdling, ear splitting scream coming from my sisters' room tears us apart.

I push away from Zagreus, and we sprint across the hall to Deme. Her door is locked but Zagreus pushes me aside and kicks the door open, splinters of old wood fall to the floor. Deme is sitting up in her bed, her eyes rolled into the back of her head so that only the whites are showing. Her mouth hangs open, but she is no longer screaming. She looks paralyzed, frozen solid. I attempt to go to her, but Zagreus grabs me by my waist and holds me back. We are both panting, hearts still beating fast. I look up at him, searching his eyes for answers.

"She's having a vision." He attempts to catch his breath, "You can't touch her until she's done." He tells me. I look back at my sister. Waiting in agony to go to her. It feels like seconds, minutes, hours, and days before Zagreus loosens his grip on me and I'm able to console my sister.

Deme is breathing uncontrollably and shaking like she is in the middle of the arctic. Her eyes are closed now, I lay her head in my lap and rub her temples gently with the tips of my fingers to calm her; my own heartbeat still rapidly beating in my chest.

"Shh..." I tell her, "It's going to be okay. It was just a vision."

"No..." She attempts, but her breathing is still out of control and tears begin to spill from her eyes. "You don't understand." She tries again.

"I don't understand what? Deme, what did you see?" I ask her.

"He is coming. Fear, violence, war, and death. The end...The end is coming."

END OF BOOK TWO

Randee Lee, professionally known as R.L. Nelson, has been writing stories as long as she could hold a pencil. What started as a childhood passion for story-telling, has become her lifelong passion. There is nothing Randee enjoys more than writing (and reading) stories that are heart-wrenching, with some humor and a hint of romance. When she's not dreaming up new stories to tell, you can find Randee spending her time with family, playing video games, painting, or binge-watching true crime dramas.

For more information visit her website www.AuthorRLnelson.com